SALLY GARDNER

Illustrated by

David Roberts

WINGS & CO

THE FAIRY DETECTIVE AGENCY

THE VANISHING
OF BILLY BUCKLE

Orion
Children's Books

First published in Great Britain in 2013
by Orion Children's Books
a division of the Orion Publishing Group Ltd
Orion House
5 Upper St Martin's Lane
London WC2H 9EA
A Hachette UK Company

1 3 5 7 9 10 8 6 4 2

A catalogue record for this book is available from the British Library.

ISBN 978 1 4440 0374 1

Printed and bound in Great Britain
by Clays Ltd, St Ives plc

The Orion Publishing Group's policy is to use papers that are natural,
renewable and recyclable products made from wood grown in sustainable
forests. The logging and manufacturing processes are expected to
conform to the environmental regulations of the country of origin.

www.orionbooks.co.uk

To Julia Paton

A dear friend who is always spot on the fishcake

SG

Chapter One

The renowned fairy detective agency, Wings & Co, had a problem. Really quite a big problem. In fact, you could say it had a ginormous problem. The giant, Billy Buckle, had vanished and, if that wasn't big enough, he had left his six-year-old daughter, Primrose, in the care of the detectives, Fidget the cat, Emily Vole and Buster Ignatius Spicer.

The trouble was that Primrose, being a giant's daughter, was growing a little taller every day. Unless the three detectives found Billy Buckle – and soon – she would be too big to go in and out of the shop. But, as Emily knew from past cases, nothing to do with fairy folk, be they witches, elves, goblins or giants, was going to be simple.

Emily Vole, the Keeper of the Keys, had inherited Wings & Co from Miss String, an enchanting old lady who had lived next door to Emily's dreadful adoptive parents, the Dashwoods. It was Miss String who had saved her from being their unpaid servant-stroke-nanny. She had taught Emily to read and write, and much more besides. During their first case together, Fidget and Emily had found the famous fairy detective, Buster Ignatius Spicer, shrunk to the size of a doll and locked in a bird cage by a goblin. Emily had bought the birdcage and freed Buster but he still felt that A) Emily shouldn't have inherited the detective agency, and B) Emily shouldn't have become Keeper of the the Keys. She wasn't a fairy and by rights it should have been his job. He was a proper fairy born and bred. But perhaps the real reason Buster was permanently grumpy was that he had been eleven for a hundred years and the only thing he didn't know about being eleven was how to become twelve.

Then there was Fidget. Emily could imagine many things but never life without dear Fidget. He was a handsome, long-haired tortoiseshell cat, one hundred and ninety centimetres tall, who had been a builder for a magician until the witch Harpella had turned him into a cat.

And there they all were, with one ginormous problem.

It had started one wet Monday when Fidget told Emily that his old mate, the giant Billy Buckle, needed someone to look after his daughter Primrose for a weekend.

'Why?' said Emily.

So many strange things had happened since Emily had first met Fidget that the idea he knew a giant didn't strike her as all that odd.

'Because he plays the bassoon in the Sad Dads' Band and they are having a reunion gig.'

'Why couldn't he take his daughter with him?' Emily had asked.

'Because of the Bog-Eyed Loader,' replied Fidget.

'The Bog-Eyed Loader,' repeated Emily.

'Yep. He lives in a cave in the Valley of Doom,' said Fidget. Fidget was seated in his favourite armchair, knitting a cotton fish-shaped hat while outside the rain poured. It was not, Emily thought, much of a summer.

'I've never heard of it. Is it near Podgy Bottom?' she asked.

'Frazzle a fishmonger! It's nowhere near here. It's in the land of the giants,' said Fidget.

'How is it that you know Billy Buckle?' asked Emily.

'Billy was a great friend of Miss String,' said Fidget.

Anything to do with the late Miss Ottoline String always had Emily's full attention.

Fidget and Miss String had first met Billy Buckle many moons ago when the fairy detectives were investigating the Case of the Missing Harp. After that, the giant had often visited them for tea, until he'd moved away.

'He did?' said Emily, impressed. She tried to imagine a giant sitting in one of Miss String's deckchairs and drinking tea out of an impossibly small tea cup. 'Where did he move to?'

'We never knew, my little ducks,' said Fidget. 'That's the thing with giants. They have very long legs. Anyway, now, out of the blue, I've heard from him.'

'How?'

'There is a postal service,' said Fidget.

'You mean letters? With stamps? Not email?'

'Well, not stamps exactly. Not email exactly.

Sometimes, my little ducks,' said Fidget kindly, 'I have to pinch myself and remember you are not a fairy.'

'Oh dear,' said Emily. 'I wish I was. It might make things easier. For a start, Buster wouldn't be so horrible to me.'

'Never mind,' said Fidget. 'I wouldn't change a squid about you.'

'What exactly is a Bog-Eyed Loader?' asked Emily.

'He is an ogre, most of the time, and fierce to boot, with a nasty habit of shape-shifting.'

'Oh,' said Emily. 'Like turning into a . . . a . . . hippopotamus?'

'Yep. That sort of thing.'

'Or . . . a fish?'

'If he did that,' said Fidget, 'I would sardine-tin him straightaway.'

A twitchy look came over Fidget's whiskers, which usually meant he felt he had answered enough questions. Emily was determined to find out more before Fidget went off in search of fishpaste sandwiches.

'So that's why Billy Buckle isn't taking his daughter.'

'Spot on the fishcake,' said Fidget. 'The Bog-Eyed

Loader has been known to take travellers prisoner. Once he caught a wizard's wife and wouldn't let her go until the wizard agreed to teach the Bog-Eyed Loader some spells. A magic spell in the hands of the Bog-Eyed Loader is a very dangerous thing indeed. There is no knowing what he might do with it.'

Emily had wanted to ask why Primrose couldn't stay with her mum if the Valley of Doom was so unsafe, and about what else a Bog-Eyed Loader could do, but she saw that Fidget was lost in fishy dreams. He wandered off, muttering to himself about fishpaste sandwiches.

She had tried to find out more about the ogre from Buster. He was sprawled on his bed looking at a magazine. He glanced up at Emily.

'Do you think my clothes look a bit old fashioned?' he said. 'Has the time has come for a revamp?'

'What do you know about the Bog-Eyed Loader?' Emily asked.

'Don't go saying his name round here. It isn't lucky,' said Buster.

'Why not?' asked Emily.

'Because he can foggle a fairy.'

'Foggle?'

'Oh,' said Buster. 'Yet another of the many things you don't know about fairies. You do know that bats make a high-pitched noise that echoes back at them so they can find their way in the dark?'

'Yes,' said Emily. 'I do, actually.' She was rather interested in bats.

'Well, fairies have the same sort of thing and the Bog-Eyed Loader can foggle it up, which isn't good.'

'You mean the fairies bang into things and can't find their way around?'

But by now Buster was bored with the subject.

'Look at these trainers,' he said. 'They're well wicked. There are gold ones and silver ones – even trainers with flashing lights. I think I would look super-cool in those.'

Emily sighed. Why wouldn't anyone tell her more about the Bog-Eyed Loader? He sounded interesting, and since they had solved the Case of the Three Pickled Herrings, not much that was interesting had happened. Life had settled down to a sleepy pace. The weather had become warmer, the trees had turned green and Buster went out flying . . . a lot.

The magic lamp, which had once belonged to the witch Harpella, but had since turned over a new leaf, now spent hours in front of the mirror shining itself and encouraging the keys to have a better hygiene programme. Emily sometimes wondered if the title Keeper of the Keys shouldn't belong to the magic lamp rather than her, for the keys never did a thing she asked them to do. Like opening drawers in the curious cabinets and returning wings to their rightful owners. They only seemed to listen to the lamp and followed it around wherever it went. As for Doughnut, the miniature dachshund, who had adopted the detectives during the Case of the Three Pickled Herrings, he slept most of the day or waited to be taken for a walk. Fidget sat knitting more and more fish scarves, hats, gloves and jumpers. He had even knitted a dress for Emily that had ended up in the shape of a fish. Emily was very proud of it and wore it quite often.

The most exciting event in ages was the arrival of Billy Buckle and Primrose. They had turned up one muggy July

evening two weeks earlier. Emily's first glimpse of Billy had been a pair of very large, red shoes at the shop's entrance. Above them were striped socks and tartan trousers. Billy was the height of the second floor, and as for Primrose, she was only just able to squeeze through the shop door.

Billy Buckle had crouched down to talk to Fidget.

'It's very decent of you, dude,' he said. 'The boys are right chuffed I am going to be there. At last the Sad Dads' Band will be back together again.'

'How long will you be gone?' Fidget had asked.

'Oh, a couple of days at the most. If it wasn't for the Bog-Eyed Loader I'd take my Primrose with me. But there you go – it just isn't safe. I can look after myself but she's only a little thing.'

He gave Primrose a kiss, told her to be good, and went on his way.

Since then there had been no sign of Billy Buckle. Fidget had made the usual enquiries and letters had been exchanged with the other Sad Dads. All that anyone knew was that Billy Buckle had played two sets with the band before leaving to pick up Primrose. Fidget had even taken an ad in *Fairy World International*. It said, simply, that anyone with any information as to the whereabouts of Billy Buckle should contact Wings & Co.

Emily had asked Fidget quietly if the Bog-Eyed Loader could be responsible. More letters flew here and there.

'Definitely not,' said Fidget. 'Billy disappeared before he made it to the Valley of Doom.'

Still no one had replied to the ad.

This, Emily had decided, was a case for Wings & Co. And they needed to solve it quickly, for Primrose was growing daily.

Chapter Two

U nexpected things often happened at Wings & Co,
but the shop was still able to spring a surprise.

It had been built on four stout iron legs and at the
end of each leg were three griffin's talons so that it could
dig its way out of its foundations and go walking if it
felt like it. Not that Emily had ever known it do so. Ever
since she had taken over the shop it had stayed firmly in
Podgy Bottom.

That Wednesday morning, she woke to find the sun
shining through her curtains, which in itself was strange,
for not much sun ever came into the dark alleyway in
Podgy Bottom, and never had she heard the sound of
waves splashing outside her bedroom window. Emily
leaped out of bed and pulled back her curtains to find the
view completely changed. She was staring at a sea that

sparkled with white-flecked waves.

This was so unexpected that for a moment she couldn't believe her eyes. She closed her curtains again, and with butterflies fluttering in her tummy, opened them for the second time. The view was still the same. Just across the road there was a beach with donkeys, and children with buckets and spades. Better still, Emily could see a pier with a big wheel on it.

'Fidget,' she called as she opened her bedroom door. 'Fidget.'

She ran down the passage and collided with the cat.

'We've moved, my little ducks,' said Fidget, lifting Emily off her feet and giving her a hug. 'The old shop has decided to go walking.' He put Emily down. 'It seems it needed a bit of holiday.'

'Oh, yippee!' cried Emily. She stopped. 'Oh, whoops. We have a case to solve. And I don't even know where we are.'

Buster came sleepily out of his bedroom.

'There is a pair of eyes looking at me through the curtains and those eyes weren't there last night.'

'We have moved to the seaside,' said Fidget.

'That still doesn't explain why two creepy eyes are looking in at me. Plus there is a terrible noise coming from outside. A noise with screams attached.'

The door on the landing flew open. The magic lamp marched out wearing a pair of sunglasses and an inflatable ring round its tummy. Behind it were the keys, all in a row.

'We are going to dip our toes in the sea,' said the magic lamp, with a skip and a hop. 'Hi-de-ho! We are on holiday!'

'Wait a mo,' said Buster. 'Salt water and an old brass lamp. Isn't that a recipe for rust?'

'Don't try to be a cloud on my sunny day,' said the lamp, walking towards the stairs, only to be sent spinning by Doughnut the dog, who had rushed up from the shop, wagging his tail.

'Oh, really,' said the magic lamp. 'Why can't that dog ever look where he's going?'

'Come on,' said Fidget. 'Get dressed and let's find out where we are.'

'Hold on a moment,' said Emily. 'Haven't we forgotten someone?'

'Who?' asked Buster.

'Primrose?' said Emily.

'Buddleia,' said Fidget. 'This puts a cod in the works. What are we going to do now?'

'What's the problem?' asked Buster.

'We need to find Billy Buckle – and fast,' said Emily. 'That's the problem. Remember? Primrose's dad is missing.'

'Oh, that,' sighed Buster. 'Not much of an investigation for a detective such as I.'

'In that case, why haven't you solved it?' asked Emily.

'Simply because there is nothing to solve,' said Buster. 'Billy Buckle met up with his chums and forgot the time. I bet he'll be back tomorrow, won't he, Fidget.'

Fidget didn't look quite so sure.

'Hmm,' he said.

'How will he find us?' said Emily. 'We have moved, if you haven't noticed.'

'Look,' said Buster, 'this is no big deal. If I was Primrose's father I would need more than a weekend away. I mean, I would need months and months and months away.'

'She is only six. I expect you were whiny when you were six,' said Emily.

'He was certainly grumpy,' said Fidget.

'No, wasn't. I was charm itself. Anyway, I don't care how old she is, she's jolly irritating. That's all I'm saying. I bet you Billy Buckle is having a rock-rolling party somewhere.'

Emily sighed. At times, working with Buster was most trying.

The guest bedroom door opened and there stood Primrose. She had a button nose and freckles, and her hair hung down in plaits. She was clinging to a sheepskin rug that she called Raggy. She was twice as tall as Emily and growing taller daily. Already there had been no end of problems on account of Primrose's size. She wasn't used to living over a small shop where she could bang her head on the ceiling. And Wings & Co was so crammed full of bits and pieces that it was very hard indeed for her not to send something or other flying.

'Where are we?' asked Primrose, rubbing her eyes.

'Um . . . the shop felt in need of a holiday,' said Fidget, 'and has taken a little walk.'

'Is that a good thing?' asked Primrose.

'Er . . . yes,' said Fidget.

'But how will my dad find us? Won't he go back to where he left me? And what then?' said Primrose.

Emily smiled weakly. 'Don't worry, Primrose,' she said. 'We have everything under control.'

At that moment the magic lamp came trotting back up the stairs from the front door.

'My day is ruined – ruined, I tell you. The front door won't open. I have pulled, I have pushed. And so have the keys. The shop has gone into lockdown.' The lamp stamped its little foot. 'Why?' he said. 'That's what I would like to know. Why?'

So would I, thought Emily.

Chapter Three

Edie Girdle closed her fortune-telling booth on the South Pier that afternoon and took herself off to the Starburst Ballroom. There, in its once-grand surroundings, she and her friend Betty Sutton, the landlady of the Mermaid Hotel, regularly took part in the tea dance. It was the treat of their week to eat cakes and trip the light fantastic in their dancing shoes.

Both ladies were striking. Edie Girdle was thin and tall with thick unruly hair and a liking for colourful clothes and jangly earrings. Betty, on the other hand, was more refined in her taste, with neatly cropped hair and a penchant for cashmere and pearls. They had been friends for as long as they could remember and had been going to the tea dance every Wednesday for the last twenty years. Since their husbands had passed away, they had danced together.

'Why should we stop?' Betty always said. 'I mean, you have to have something to look forward to, don't you?'

Edie couldn't have agreed more.

The ballroom had a shiny, wooden dance floor surrounded by little tables and chairs where tea was served to the dancers. At one end stood the stage with its red plush velvet curtains. They, like everything else, had seen better days. Nevertheless, Morris Flipwinkle sat happily playing the Starburst Ballroom's famous Wurlitzer. The organ, painted white and red, still sounded as good as the day it was built, back in the 1920s.

'You know,' Edie had once said to Betty, 'I hadn't a clue what a Wurlitzer was before I came to Puddliepool-on-Sea. I mean, I thought it was a fairground ride, not an organ with buttons and pedals.'

'Eee . . .' said Betty. 'You weren't far off the mark, love. It sounds to me like a merry-go-round playing the waltz.'

It was after several whirls on the dance floor that they sat down to have their tea.

'How're the bookings going at the hotel?' asked Edie.

'Fully booked,' said Betty. 'And with only one guest, a gentleman.'

'No – never! And he's taken all of your five rooms?'

'The whole caboodle.'

'Who is he?' asked Edie.

'His name's Mr Belvale,' said Betty. 'He's taken over the Starburst Amusement Park.' She lowered her voice to a whisper. 'I tell you this, Edie, love, the man gives me the creeps.'

'Why?'

'I don't rightly know, love,' said Betty. 'There's something about him. He keeps leaving the windows wide open in the master suite. The rain came in and ruined the carpet. It had to be replaced. I told him politely what had happened and he just said to add it to his bill. Then the other day I found a blooming seagull perched on top of the camels – it gave me the fright of my life.'

The Mermaid Hotel was known for its themed bedrooms. The Oasis Suite, as Betty called it, had been decorated with palm tree curtains, a sandy-coloured

carpet and a cluster of three wooden camels next to
the bed.

'That seagull had pooed everywhere. It took hours to
clean it up,' said Betty.

'It sounds to me as though Mr Belvale's just absent
minded,' said Edie.

'No,' said Betty. 'There's something else.'

Morris Flipwinkle started to play his last number.
At the end of his set, he and the famous Wurlitzer would
sink below the stage.

'Come on,' said Betty. 'Let's have this dance. It'll be
that stuck-up Johnny Carmichael on next.'

Johnny Carmichael played the second shift. None of
the regulars liked him much. Morris Flipwinkle was, without
doubt, their favourite.

Edie stepped on Betty's toe.

'Ouch,' said Betty. 'Edie, your heart's not in it today.'

'It's because the sea is flat,' said Edie.

Betty looked worriedly at her friend. It wasn't like Edie
to go all mystic on her.

'We live in Puddliepool-on-Sea. The sea is often flat,'

said Betty. 'It has to do with tides, the moon, that sort of thing. Are you all right, love? The sea being flat has never worried you before.'

'No, Betty, don't be daft. I'm not talking about the waves and the sea. I'm talking about the Wurlitzer. Listen . . . the note C. I think . . .' said Edie, but Betty couldn't hear what Edie thought.

A loud rumble and a muted scream came from under the floor where every ten minutes the ghost train ride rattled the old ballroom.

'You what?' said Betty.

It was then, to her friend's horror, that the strangest thing happened. Edie Girdle vanished into thin air.

'I was left cha-cha-chaing with no one,' Betty later told Mr Trickett, the owner of the ballroom. She clicked her fingers to show him just how fast her friend had disappeared. 'We have to find her.'

'Yes, of course,' said Mr Trickett.

But Mr Trickett hadn't been called from his office to

discuss the sudden disappearance of Edie Girdle. No.
He was there on a much more serious matter. His Wurlitzer
player, Johnny Carmichael, had just been found with a
knife sticking out of the back of his dinner jacket, dead
as dead could be. And Morris Flipwinkle was nowhere to
be seen.

Chapter Four

A little earlier that same afternoon, the shop door of Wings & Co had silently opened and the fairy detectives were free to explore. The sign on the side of a tram told Emily and Fidget where they were. 'Welcome,' it said, 'to Puddliepool-on-Sea.'

'How far is Puddliepool-on-Sea from Podgy Bottom?' asked Primrose, her eyes welling with tears.

'Search my catnip,' said Fidget.

'Not all that far,' said Emily, giving Primrose's hand a little squeeze. 'Is it, Buster?'

Buster wasn't listening – or looking, for that matter. He was staring up at the shop and into the sky beyond, his eyes glazed in wonder.

'Wowzer!' he said over and over again. 'Wowzer! Listen to them scream!'

Emily, Fidget and Primrose turned to see exactly what it was that Buster was looking at. Behind the shop was a sculpture of twisted metal rails. On it ran the lozenge of an open-topped train, filled with shrieking humans.

'What is it?' asked Emily, as the train went whizzing up the rails to the highest point. To Emily's horror, it then hurtled ever downwards, followed by a trail of screams.

'It's a big dipper,' said Buster. 'A glorious big dipper. Better known as a roller coaster and I am going to ride on it for ever and ever.'

'Hold on a mo, my old minnow, you can't go swimming off just like that,' said Fidget.

'I can. And I will,' said Buster, unfolding his wings.

He began to rise up from the pavement and nearly hit a low-flying seagull.

'Oh, really,' said Emily. 'Primrose – stop him, please.'

Primrose quickly raised her hand in the air and pulled Buster down by his ankle. On the other side of the street a family had stopped to stare at them.

'Now look what you've done,' said Emily.

The little boy watched Buster with his mouth open.

'Look, look, Mum,' he said. 'There's a real fairy.'

'I know, love,' said his mum. 'You see all sorts by the seaside.'

'Oh dear,' said Emily.

'Don't worry, my little ducks,' said Fidget. 'We'll fit in here like piranhas in a goldfish bowl.'

'You need to loosen up, Emily,' said Buster. 'We're on holiday.'

'No, we're not. We're in the middle of an investigation and we have no leads. And now we're somewhere we don't know.'

'You have a point, my little ducks,' said Fidget. 'But in all its years the shop has never got up and moved without a good reason. What the reason is this time, I don't know, but I have a tail fin of a feeling that we are about to find out.'

At that moment the magic lamp popped its spout out of the shop door.

'Oh, do come quickly, dear mistress,' it said. 'There are shenanigans going on and they are messy.'

Buster seized his chance and flew away while Emily,

Fidget and Primrose rushed back inside the shop,

The keys were flying about wildly, knocking things over and upsetting the pictures on the wall. Doughnut was hiding under the counter, his tail between his legs.

'I have tried to make them stop,' said the magic lamp, throwing up its hands in one of its many theatrical gestures. 'I have tried, but will they listen to me? No. Only you, dear, dear mistress, can bring order to this chaos.'

Just then the keys drew up in formation near the curious cabinets.

'Get down, Fidget,' shouted Emily. 'I think they mean to attack us.' Fidget and Primrose hid behind the door that led to the stairs. Emily and the magic lamp found safety with Doughnut under the counter.

'What the tuna paste is going on?' said Fidget as the keys gathered like a swarm of bees in the corner.

For one dreadful moment Emily thought they were about to fly out of the shop. She crawled across the floor and slammed the door shut as low-flying keys swooped down on her.

There was nothing to do but tackle the problem head on. She was, after all, the Keeper of the Keys. Emily stood up.

'Stop this,' she said firmly. 'Just behave yourselves.'

With a great clatter the keys fell to the wooden floor, not one of them moving, their metal all floppy. From behind Emily came the sound of breaking glass.

'Oh no!' shouted the magic lamp. One of the keys had thrown itself at the window and broken through. 'Come back! Leave it, it's not worth it!'

The key seemed to be aiming at something outside. Emily rushed to the shop door just in time to see a fluttering of feathers and the key lying on the pavement. It looked in a bad way.

'Cyril, what have you done?' wailed the magic lamp.

'Cyril?' said Emily, opening the door. 'How do you know that key is called Cyril?'

It ran out and collected Cyril, lifting up the floppy key in its little arms and bringing him back into the shop.

'You may be the Keeper of the Keys,' the lamp said to Emily, 'but to me they are more than just a bunch of ironmongery. They are my friends.'

The magic lamp screamed. All its dear friends were out cold. It knelt down and laid Cyril next to them.

'Don't leave me!' the lamp cried. 'Don't leave me all on my own!'

'Rollmop me a herring,' said Fidget. 'I've never seen the keys do that before.'

Emily thought afterwards that if the magic lamp hadn't been having one of its more dramatic turns she would have noticed then that two of the curious cabinet drawers were open. But at that moment something went whizz-bang-wallop and the shop filled with thick, bluish smoke. Fidget and Emily couldn't see a thing. Snatches of music wafted in and out, and sparks of colour flashed on and off.

'Betty? Where are you, love?' a woman's voice said.

'What's going on? Where am I?' said a man's voice.

'Only one . . . after all this time,' said the woman.

'Who are you?' called Fidget, still unable to see a thing.

There was a crashing of china, a scurrying of feet, a tinkling of the bell and the shop door slammed shut.

'Well, lean on a limpet,' said Fidget. 'Whatever next?'

Chapter Five

James Cardwell was sitting in his office on the top floor of New Scotland Yard trying to piece together exactly what had happened during the Bond Street jewellery robbery.

It had taken place the previous week in broad daylight at twelve-thirty when the street had been packed with shoppers. The sheer cheek and scale of the robbery had stunned onlookers and the police alike. From the eye-witness accounts that Detective Cardwell had collected, and from CCTV cameras and video taken on mobile phones, the culprits appeared to be two old ladies, both on mobility scooters. They had been spotted earlier that morning near Oxford Circus tube station, before heading towards Bond Street. Witnesses said they'd been wearing colourful scarves and sunglasses, and from the back of each mobility scooter a flag flew. On their baskets at the front were arrangements of plastic flowers.

Bond Street had been busier than usual on account of the Galaxy Diamond. For one week only, it was being displayed in the shop window of Myrtle & Finch Jewellers. The store had its own security guards and special reinforced glass had been installed in the shop window. The jeweller's owners, who lived in Dubai, were certain that the Galaxy Diamond – worth seven million pounds – was as safe as if it were in a bank vault.

But they hadn't taken into account the little old ladies on their mobility scooters. The women arrived at the shop and barged their way through to the front of the crowd to stare at the diamond, which was mounted on a velvet cushion.

It was at this point that one of the old ladies started to wave her umbrella above her head, shouting at the top of her voice for everyone to clear off. The two security guards rushed forward to see what the hullabaloo was about. But neither man remembered a thing after being jabbed in the leg with the end of the umbrella. One of the old ladies stood up and, swinging her handbag as if it were a ball and chain, smashed it through the shop window, shattering the reinforced glass with ease and setting off the alarm system. The other old lady grabbed the Galaxy Diamond and in the chaos that followed the two culprits escaped on their pimped-up mobility scooters.

So far the CCTV footage had given no clues to the true identities of the two thieves. It had shown them going off at 40 mph, in the direction of Piccadilly Circus. After that, there was no trace of them. And no trace of the diamond either. The mobility scooters had eventually been found abandoned in Poland Street Car Park along with a lead-lined handbag.

It was one of the toughest cases Detective Cardwell could remember in a long time. He swivelled round in his chair as a smartly dressed woman with blonde, bobbed hair popped her head round the door.

'Here they are,' she said, handing him a USB stick. 'Files on nearly all the jewel thieves in the world for you to go through.'

James smiled weakly.

'By any chance, are there two little old ladies among them?'

'Not that I know of,' said Poppy. 'No breakthrough, then?' she asked kindly. 'I suppose no one suspects little old ladies of doing anything wrong.'

'No,' said Detective Cardwell. Poppy was new on his team and whenever she came into a room he felt his heart flutter that little bit faster. It was the first time in a long, long while.

'If anyone can catch them, I'm sure it's you,' she said, as she closed the door behind her.

James sighed. He knew he could never go out with someone who wasn't like him. It just wouldn't work.

The phone rang.

'Sorry to disturb you, sir,' said a voice with a Northern accent. 'This is Sergeant Binns, Puddliepool-on-Sea Police Station. We have apprehended a youngster by the name of Buster Ignatius Spicer. He says you know him.'

'What's this all about, Sergeant?' asked Detective Cardwell.

'The lad in question has been arrested due to an

incident involving the roller coaster ride at the Starburst Amusement Park.'

James Cardwell sighed again. 'I'll be there as quickly as I can,' he said.

He made sure that the office door was closed before opening the window. London looked hot and grey below. Detective Cardwell took off his jacket and climbed carefully on to the window ledge. He unfolded his wings and stretched them out. It was good to feel the wind in them. Then he pushed himself off the top of New Scotland Yard and flew up into the sky, heading north to Puddliepool-on-Sea.

Chapter Six

Buster was in a terrible grump by the time he and James Cardwell arrived back at Wings & Co. Life, he had decided, was unfair, very unfair indeed. James had read him the Fairy Code of Conduct. There was, he thought, no need for that. Who did James think he was? A hundred years ago he had been Buster's best friend and now, just because he'd grown up, wore a suit and was a detective at Scotland Yard, he thought he had the right to tell *him*, Buster Ignatius Spicer, how to behave. Buster was so lost in the red fog of his own bad temper that he didn't notice the shattered glass in the front door of the fairy detective agency.

Inside the old shop it looked as if a troop of elephants had taken up dancing lessons. A chair knocked over, books lying open on the floor, Fidget's favourite tea mug broken. Detective Cardwell had never seen the shop in such a state.

'Buddleia. It's that girl again,' said Buster. 'She only has to do a hop and a skip and all the pictures fall off the walls. That's the trouble with girls – always messing things up.'

The magic lamp hurried out from behind the counter carrying a first aid bag.

'It's a calamity, I tell you,' it cried. 'A terrible calamity!'

'What's going on?' asked James Cardwell.

'No time,' said the lamp and skedaddled.

'Hello,' called James. 'Is anyone here?'

Fidget came down the stairs followed by Emily, who rushed up to James and gave him a hug.

'I'm so pleased you are here,' she said. 'We're in a terrible mess.'

'Jimmy, my old cod,' said Fidget.

'Have you been robbed?' asked Detective Cardwell.

'Sort of,' said Emily. 'But we can't be sure. The shop went walking and . . .' Seeing Buster, she stopped. 'So you decided to come back? I thought you were going to ride on the roller coaster for ever and ever.'

'He's grounded,' said James Cardwell firmly.

'Grounded as in not allowed to fly?'

'Correct,' said James. 'For the time being at least.'

'Why?' asked Emily. 'What's he done?'

'Don't answer that, James,' said Buster. 'It's none of her business. And anyway, a century ago, you would've been up there with me. Now you're so grown up and boring. I've had enough of all of you.'

'All right, old sprat,' Fidget called as Buster went stomping upstairs. 'So are you resigning from being a detective?'

'No,' said Buster.

'Then wake up and smell the fish fingers,' said Fidget. 'If you can be bothered to look around you, you might notice that we are in a bit of a predicament.'

'A what?' said Buster.

'A pre-dic-a-ment,' said Fidget. 'A pickle, in other words.'

The red fog began to clear. Buster sighed and turned round, nearly tripping up the magic lamp.

'Watch where you're going,' said the lamp. It was

carrying one of the keys in its arms. It hung down, all floppy. 'Can't you see Rory is at death's door?'

'I'm sorry,' said Buster. 'I got carried away. But I'm here now.'

'About time too,' said Emily.

'What's happened? And what are you doing in Puddliepool-on-Sea in the first place?' asked Detective Cardwell.

Emily wished she knew the answer to that question. And she wished she knew what was wrong with the keys. There was no manual on being Keeper and Buster had once told her that it came naturally to those who were chosen. She was beginning to feel that everything was out of control.

It was Fidget who explained how the shop had moved in the night then gone into lockdown. How the keys had turned on them, how one – Cyril – had broken the glass in the front door and flown out. How, when the smoke cleared, another – Rory – was found in a drawer . . .

'. . . just hanging there, all droopy, not like metal at all,' said Emily. 'And that's not the worst of it.'

'Squat on a squid,' said Fidget. 'Not the worst of it by a long fishing rod.' He took James Cardwell to the curious cabinets, where two of the drawers had been opened and in each drawer only one wing remained. 'Never,' said Fidget gravely, 'have I seen a sight as fishy as this.'

It occurred to Buster that perhaps it all had something to do with the giant girl.

'Is Primrose OK?' he asked.

'Primrose?' interrupted James. 'You don't mean Billy Buckle's daughter? What's she doing here?'

This time it was Emily who filled James Cardwell in.

When she had finished, James asked, 'Where's Primrose now?'

'Upstairs with Doughnut,' said Emily. 'Sleeping. It must be very tiring, growing so fast. In fact we will be in quite a predicament if she keeps on growing. As it is she has to bend double to go through the doors and she can't sit on the chairs and if she waves her arms about things fall off walls.' Emily lowered her voice. 'I don't think the shop was designed for giant's daughters.'

'Definitely not,' said James. 'And two weeks is too long,

far too long. Billy Buckle is a very responsible father. He would never abandon her on purpose. Maybe it's because of Primrose that the shop moved. But why here?'

'Can you help us?' Emily asked. 'Perhaps this case is beyond us.'

'Speak for yourself,' said Buster. 'I'm just as old as James and have been a detective just as long.'

'I would help if I could,' said James. 'But I must go back to London. I have a robbery to deal with. I will see what I can find out from my end and let you know.'

They all trooped up to the attic and watched James fly off into the blue sky.

'It would be good if he could stay,' Emily said sadly.

'I agree, my little ducks,' said Fidget.

'When I was at the police station,' said Buster, 'I had tea and ginger snaps with Sergeant Binns.'

'It's amazing he didn't hit you round the ear with a kipper,' said Fidget. 'You must have caused no end of trouble if Jimmy had to fly up here to sort it out.'

'As I was saying,' said Buster, ignoring Fidget, 'Sergeant Binns told me there had been a murder at the Starburst

Ballroom. The victim was Johnny Carmichael, one of the Wurlitzer players. James wanted to see his picture. He was so interested that he asked for a copy to take back with him to Scotland Yard.'

'And what's that to do with anything?' said Emily.

'I'm just trying to be nice and explain why James can't stay.'

'Nice?' said Emily. 'Well, it would be nice if you took the disappearance of Billy Buckle more seriously, not to mention the disaster with the keys.'

'I do,' said Buster. 'I do take it all seriously. Anyway, aren't you supposed to be the Keeper of the Keys?'

'All right,' said Emily. 'I am. And I admit I don't know what to do about them.'

What she didn't admit was that she felt a bit wobbly. She liked things to be solid. She liked it when the keys and the shop behaved themselves. The idea that the shop might wander off again worried her greatly. What if she was left behind? What if she could never find Wings & Co? She might be returned to Cherryfield Orphanage, or worse still to her dreadful adoptive parents, Ronald and Daisy

Dashwood. The thought made her tummy feel fluttery. It was tough not having parents but it would be even tougher if there was no Fidget to look out for her.

Chapter Seven

In the early morning light, the town of Puddliepool-on-Sea shimmered in a heat haze. The sun, a sleepy yellow balloon, rose lazily into the sky. The sand was all golden and the sea a greyish blue with gentle waves that splashed against the shore. Everything was ready and waiting for the invasion of families, deckchairs, sandcastles, donkey rides and ice creams.

This was, without doubt, Edie Girdle's favourite time of day, before the crowds were up and doing, when the morning looked washed and freshly hung out to dry. Which was more than she could say about herself.

Edie sat in Betty's kitchen at the Mermaid Hotel, wrapped in a mac. It hadn't been easy to hide her one and only wing. She had forgotten what her wings looked like, it had been such an age since she had last seen them. Now she wasn't even certain if a bath was a good idea or not. Perhaps a shower would be better. How was she to know? Plumbing had moved on, and so had the world, and she had got used to being without her wings, especially after the car was invented. And now you could fly so cheaply here and there, they were somewhat unnecessary. Still, it had been a terrible shock to find she only had one of the things. What was she to do with only one wing? Something, she thought miserably, had gone very wrong. One minute she was on the dance floor, the next – hey presto – she was inside that old shop. What did they used to call it? It was such a long time since she had left her wings there. Wings – yes, that was it, Wings & Co.

At the same time that sunny morning, Blinky Belvale, the Mermaid Hotel's one and only guest, was sitting in the dining room eating his breakfast: two fried eggs, three rashers of bacon, four sausages, five slices of black pudding, six fried tomatoes, seven potato cakes, ten mushrooms, and a mountain of white buttered toast.

He was a big man with eyes that looked as if they could pop out of their sockets at any minute. He was dressed in an ill-fitting checked suit of a slime-green colour. On his head was perched, as always, a small pork-pie hat. As he munched away he could hear the Mermaid's landlady talking to someone in the kitchen.

Betty finished washing the frying pan and sat down next to Edie.

'Now tell me, love, what happened to you? Are you all right? You sounded dreadful when you called me last night.' She stopped and looked at her friend. 'Why are you wearing a mac? It's going to be a blooming scorcher. You'll be as hot as a boiled lobster in that.'

'Silly, I know,' said Edie. 'I'm feeling a little chilly.'

'Eee, love,' said Betty, 'you should go home and rest. Come to think of it, you do look a bit peaky. It's the shock of what happened at the ballroom. Though to tell you the truth, I still don't understand how you vanished.'

Edie smiled weakly and mumbled something into her tea. She picked up the newspaper and read the headline. 'THE MYSTERY OF THE FLYING BOY'. Underneath was a photograph of a boy apparently flying to the top of the roller coaster.

'Trick photography, that's all,' said Betty.

No, it's not, thought Edie. I am sure I know that lad from old. That's Buster Ignatius Spicer, the famous fairy detective, if my memory isn't failing me. What's he doing in Puddliepool-on-Sea?

Betty pointed to the story above.

'MURDER ON THE DANCE FLOOR'.

'But it wasn't,' said Betty.

'What wasn't?' said Edie.

'The murder didn't take place on the dance floor. Johnny Carmichael was bumped off under the stage, so I heard.'

Edie's heart sank as she read the paper. 'It says here that Morris Flipwinkle is wanted in connection with the murder.'

'Yes, a warrant has been issued for his arrest,' said Betty.

'Never,' said Edie. 'Not our Morris. He came to me for a consultation, you know. He's a real gentleman. I tell you, they have the wrong man. Morris Flipwinkle wouldn't hurt a . . . MOUSE!'

Betty let out a squeal and shot to her feet. Sure enough, in the corner of the kitchen was a mouse, sitting there as bold as brass, as if listening to what was being said.

'Oh, Edie, I've never had a mouse in my kitchen, not in thirty years in this business.'

'Don't worry,' said Edie. 'It most probably came through the cat flap.'

Betty sat down.

'I feel quite faint. What's happening? First that seagull and now . . .'

Edie took a broom and chased the mouse out of the back door.

'You don't think Mr Belvale heard that?' said Betty.

'No,' said Edie.

'Mrs Sutton,' shouted Blinky Belvale, making them both jump.

Betty patted down her apron and stuck her head through the hatch to the dining room.

'Yes, Mr Belvale,' she said. 'Is there anything else you would like? A pot of tea?'

'Another breakfast,' said Mr Belvale.

'Is that wise?' said Betty. 'I mean, you've had three Full Englishes already.'

'Is that a problem?' said Blinky Belvale, his eyes flashing.

'Not at all,' said Betty.

'No toast this time, just pancakes. And make that twenty-one of them – with a large jug of maple syrup.'

Betty withdrew her head from the hatch.

'Another breakfast?' said Edie as Betty put the frying pan back on the stove.

'I wonder,' said Betty to her friend as she poured the pancake mixture, 'if you couldn't have a look into that crystal ball of yours and see what you can find out about that murder?'

'I could,' said Edie.

'And while you're about it, love,' whispered Betty, 'would you have a little peek and see what you can find out about . . .' she mouthed, '. . . Blinky Belvale.'

Chapter Eight

It was exactly ten past ten when Blinky Belvale arrived at his new office in the Starburst Amusement Park. He had bought the amusement park less than two months before and had grand plans for it, all of which were being held up by Mr Trickett. The owner of the Starburst Ballroom refused to sell the old place to him. No one refuses Blinky Belvale anything, thought Blinky, as Mr Trickett would soon find out to his cost. He settled down at his shiny desk to read the local newspaper. 'MURDER ON THE DANCE FLOOR' seemed to be the headline of the day.

'That will do it nicely,' chuckled Blinky Belvale. 'I can't see any bank lending money to Mr Trickett now. He'll be forced to sell to me and there is nowt he can do about it.'

Blinky rubbed his hands together. Then an item on page two caught his eye. 'FORTUNE-TELLER VANISHES, REAPPEARS THREE HOURS LATER'. He read on. Edie Girdle. That was the old bat who was gossiping in the kitchen with Mrs Sutton.

'I don't like gossip,' said Blinky Belvale to himself. 'Gossip should stay firmly in the gob and not be spread about like muck. Neither do I like fortune-tellers who go looking in crystal balls and seeing what they shouldn't.'

Last of all, he glanced at the national papers. They were still on about the robbery in Bond Street. No closer to finding the culprits. There was a picture of the detective in charge of the case. Cardwell. Blinky put on his round glasses to study the article more closely. They had the effect of making his eyes look enormous in his head.

'Cheryl!' he bellowed.

Cheryl Spike was his personal assistant. He had chosen her from a long list of applicants, all far more suited to the job of personal assistant than she was, but Blinky Belvale liked women with a bit of muscle on them. And Cheryl Spike certainly had muscles. She had been the Women's

Wrestling Champion of Puddliepool-on-Sea before she was disqualified for not only biting off her opponent's ear but also swallowing it.

She was dressed today, as always, in ex-army uniform over which she wore an orange day-glo vest. Her hair, dyed black, was white at the roots, and she had a smile that would curdle milk.

'Did you read about this murder at the Starburst Ballroom?' Blinky Belvale asked her, showing her the paper.

'Yes,' said Cheryl. Her voice was very low, so low that it dragged itself across the floor. 'He got what was coming to him, that's what I say.'

Blinky looked up.

'You knew this Johnny Carmichael, then?'

'Might've done. Might not,' said Cheryl, the end of her nose going red.

She sniffed.

'Where's The Toad?' asked Blinky. 'I want him here.'

The Toad was Cheryl's little brother, though they looked as different as fish from sheep, The Toad being stick thin apart from a round belly. He was always chewing bubblegum, and when he blew bubbles he looked like a toad they'd once seen in a nature programme on the telly.

Cheryl wiped her nose on her sleeve and mumbled into her walkie-talkie.

'Spike calling Toad. Come in, Toad.' She waited. 'He's not answering,' she said to her boss.

'Then you'd better find him, hadn't you?' said Blinky Belvale. 'Before I lose my temper.'

Cheryl looked worried by that idea.

'There is work to be done,' continued Blinky. 'And I don't like to be kept waiting.'

'Work such as breaking arms and bending legs, Mr B?' asked Cheryl.

'Sort of,' said Blinky. 'First, get Trickett on the phone. And then find The Toad.'

Cheryl dialled the number and handed the receiver to her boss. She picked up the walkie-talkie again and left the room.

'Mr Trickett. Blinky Belvale here. I would say, "Good morning", but it's not a good morning for you, is it?'

There was a whimper at the other end of the phone.

'You could solve all your problems by selling me the Starburst Ballroom.'

'No,' came the nervous reply. 'I've told you. The ballroom is not for sale.'

Blinky Belvale leaned back in his chair and snorted.

'And I tell you, Mr Trickett. I tell you once, I won't tell you twice. If I have to tell you three times, you will regret it. Take the money and scarper. Do I make myself clear?'

'I'm not selling,' said Mr Trickett. 'And that's my last word.'

'A pity,' said Blinky Belvale. 'A big – and terrible – pity.'

He slammed down the phone.

'Cheryl,' he called.

Cheryl and The Toad both tried to come in through the office door at the same time and got stuck.

'Stop the mucking about and get in here,' said Blinky Belvale. His employees stood to attention in front of his desk. 'Now listen to me. I need something smashed.'

Cheryl's face lit up lumpily.

'Smashing things is just up my street, Mr B, with door

knockers on. Who? Where? What?' she asked with a snarl
of which a pitbull terrier would be proud.

'The Who of it is a fortune-teller called Edie Girdle.
The Where of it is her booth on South Pier. The What of it
is her crystal ball.'

Chapter Nine

Emily had managed to find the library, which was no small feat, for the shop had a habit of hiding rooms or shrinking them. It had also been known to change its layout and, every now and then, even change its decor.

So it was with a sense of relief that she pushed open a door to see Fidget sitting at a desk studying a huge, leather-bound book.

That summer, before Billy Buckle had turned up, Emily had been helping Fidget learn to read again. He had been able to once when he had worked for the old magician who had designed the shop, but since being turned into a cat he had somewhat lost interest. Now, along with knitting, reading was high on the list of things Fidget liked doing. Not quite as high as eating fishpaste sandwiches but then nothing much was.

Fluttering around him were thin, flighty books, some dancing from one shelf to another. Most of the novels were looking serious as they watched two history books on war having a fight. Emily went over to the books and sorted it out. It was just that they should never have been put next to each other.

Emily loved books, even quarrelsome ones, but especially books with pictures in them. Lots and lots, so that the pages weren't too thick with words. There were no pictures in the book that Fidget was busily studying.

'What are you doing?' asked Emily.

'Trying to work out who the owners of the half-pairs of wings are,' said Fidget.

Emily stared at the list of names.

'What do the crosses mean?' she asked.

'They belong to those fairies who can't read or write,' said Fidget.

'Wouldn't it be better,' said Emily, 'if we put all these names in a computer file? Including the crosses, of course.'

Fidget thought for a moment then said, 'Will the names fade on the screen?'

'No,' said Emily.

'Then how would we know which fairy has been back to collect his or her wings?'

'Can't we just put a line through their names?'

'Buddleia,' said Fidget. 'I hadn't thought of that.'

'Do you think there might be book here about the habits and pastimes of giants?' asked Emily.

'Shush,' said Fidget, as Primrose came in carrying Doughnut. They both looked miserable, Doughnut because he had been dressed up in a tutu and had a hat on his head, Primrose because she missed her dad and wanted to go home.

'Daddy should have come back to collect me by now,' said Primrose. 'I mean, he would never just leave me here, I know he wouldn't. He promised. You can't break a promise, never, ever, ever.'

Oh no, thought Emily, seeing Primrose's lower lip begin to wobble. The last time she had cried she had left puddles of tears everywhere and it had taken a pail and a mop to clear them up. There really was no end to the trouble caused by living with a growing giantess. Her bed had broken two nights ago and yesterday she had used seventeen towels to dry herself after her shower. The cereal dishes didn't hold enough cornflakes to satisfy her appetite and this morning Fidget had to give her a washing-up bowlful. She was eating them out of house and home.

'Let's go downstairs,' said Emily brightly.

'I want my daddy,' said Primrose, tears welling in her eyes.

'Why don't we call your mum?' said Emily. 'Do you have her number?'

Primrose began to wail.

'Oh dear,' said Emily.

'Best not to mention Mum,' whispered Fidget. 'She left for India with her lady friend. They've gone to find themselves.'

Emily took Primrose's hand. 'I know how you feel – sort of.'

'You do?' said Primrose.

'Yes, I think so. Because my parents left me behind in a hatbox at Stansted Airport.'

Fidget said, 'I'd let that particular fish off the hook if I were you, my little ducks.'

'You mean they didn't come back, ever?' said Primrose.

'I'm sure they meant to,' said Emily. 'But . . . I found Fidget – or rather Fidget found me.'

'I want my daddy,' wailed Primrose. 'I want to go home.'

Fidget put his paw on Primrose's arm and handed her a handkerchief.

'I know your dad would never leave you. He's got a bit lost, that's all, and we're doing everything we can to find him.'

'What do you mean – lost?' said Primrose, blowing her nose into Fidget's red and white spotted hankie.

'Er, well . . .' said Fidget. Doughnut gazed up at him sadly. 'Um . . . I think we should go and buy some ice creams and build a sandcastle. Paddle in the sea, that sort of thing.'

Primrose brightened a little.

'When will he be here, my daddy?'

'Soon, very soon, I'm sure of it,' said Fidget. 'In less than a twirl of a cat's whisker.'

Doughnut ran out of the library, trailing the tutu and hat behind him, followed by a slightly more cheerful Primrose.

When they had left, Emily turned to Fidget.

'Do you think that's what my parents did?' she asked.

'What, my little ducks?'

'Went off to find themselves, like Primrose's mum?'

'No,' said Fidget. He stood up and gave Emily a big hug.

'So maybe I will never know who they are?'

'Maybe not,' said Fidget. 'But you can never tell what's round the corner.'

Emily took a deep breath and told Fidget what had been worrying her. Since she had drawn back the curtains and found they were no longer in Podgy Bottom an unsettling thought wouldn't leave her: that one day the shop might wander off without her and she would be left all alone in the world.

'That will never, ever happen,' said Fidget. 'As long as there are fishes in the sea, I will always be with you. Always.'

Emily felt a tear roll down her face. She wasn't

at all keen on tears. They could be seen as soppy, especially by Buster.

'Now, ice creams all round,' said Fidget, taking her hand in his paw.

They went downstairs.

'Where are you going?' asked Buster, sticking his head out of his bedroom.

'To the beach,' said Emily.

'Oh, goody-gumdrops. I'll come too.'

Emily rather hoped he wouldn't. Buster was very good at putting a crease in the day. But he followed them down.

'Oh, leave me behind, then,' shouted the magic lamp from the landing. 'That's right! Just go off and have fun while I look after the sick keys.'

'Come with us,' said Emily.

'I can't. I have a shop to run. Someone has to stay behind while you're out enjoying yourselves,' said the magic lamp. 'I would have expected better of you, dear mistress, than to leave me like this. Have you even thought about the keys?'

'Yes, she has,' said Fidget as he gathered together

inflatable rings, towels, suncream and hats. 'Let's go. We all need fresh air and Primrose needs a bit of fun.'

'Is this a good idea?' said Emily. 'I mean, we will stand out.'

'My little ducks,' said Fidget firmly, 'half the people we bump into don't believe in magic and they are not going to change their minds because they see a talking cat and a giant's daughter. We are off to the beach with Primrose and that's the end of it.'

Chapter Ten

Edie left the Mermaid Hotel promising Betty that she would go home and rest. But she couldn't, not with the police out searching for Morris Flipwinkle. She knew it was silly, nevertheless she felt somewhat responsible. Morris had come to see her just two weeks ago. He had wanted her to look in her crystal ball and tell him if he was going to be famous.

Unlike many in the fortune-telling business, Edie really did have second sight and she was a fairy to boot. She had been born with the gift of seeing what the future held in her magic crystal ball and it wasn't always a pretty picture. She had to be very careful what she said to her clients. The art was to look on the sunny side of people's lives, avoiding the shadows.

She had felt a bit of a failure when it came to Morris,

for she had indeed looked into her crystal ball as he had asked, and it had gone all misty. She hadn't been able to see a blooming thing. That had never happened to her before. It had almost hurt her eyes. When she did at last see something it made no sense. A skeleton, a seagull and a diamond. Quite what they had to do with Morris she had no idea, and now, with the news of the diamond theft in London and the murder of Johnny Carmichael, she wondered if her powers were failing her.

She started to walk a little faster as she passed the big wheel on the pier, heading towards her booth. She would have another good look in her crystal ball and see if she could sort out this mess.

Overhead, seagulls wheeled and squealed. Edie wasn't fond of the birds. They were very loud and they seemed to be getting larger and fatter as the years went by. Only two days ago one of them had swooped down and stolen her sandwich. A liability, that's what they were.

At the end of the South Pier was Edie's booth. She unlocked the door. The booth had a warming scent of rose petals to it and was draped with star-covered cloth so that it looked like the inside of an Aladdin's cave. There wasn't much furniture, just a table and two chairs. The main feature of the room was Edie's magnificent crystal ball, covered with a velvet cloth.

Edie took off her mac and hung it on a hook, then wrapped an enormous shawl round her shoulders to cover her one wing. She sat down and gazed into the ball. Who killed Johnny Carmichael? And who is Blinky Belvale? And why did I only get one wing back?

Outside, the seagulls flew along the promenade and there, not far away, Fidget, Primrose, Doughnut the dog, Emily and Buster were crossing the road, avoiding the horse-drawn carriages and trams. It was only when Buster looked over the rail at the beach below that he remembered why he didn't like sand.

The last time he had become involved with the stuff, possibly in the Sahara Desert, it had got between his toes and made his shoes gritty and his socks impossible.

'Fidget,' said Buster, as Emily and Primrose ran down the steps to the beach, Doughnut at their heels, 'I think I'll have a look round.'

'All right, my old sprat,' said Fidget, whose mind was on seafood and fish.

Buster wandered off, taking in his surroundings. Wings & Co had plonked itself down in a row of brightly coloured shops. The eyes that had stared at him through his bedroom window that morning were painted on the shop wall next door, he discovered. It was a sweet shop. Underneath the eyes was an advertisement for an exciting new attraction in the ghost train. 'MUST BE SEEN TO BE BELIEVED', it said. Above the shops rose the steel net of the roller coaster. This was nearly too much for Buster. It was very hard being grounded, he thought miserably. He longed to go on the roller coaster again, but he had promised James he wouldn't and, after all, James was his oldest friend. And a promise is a promise.

Then Buster saw the big wheel. It was turning slowly, round and round, on the pier that stretched out into the sea.

'I could go on that,' Buster said to himself. 'I mean, it isn't a roller coaster and if I just sit there and don't fly off then nothing can possibly go wrong.'

He felt himself being drawn towards the big wheel by a magnetic force. Buster decided that he hadn't any choice in the matter. It wasn't his fault, his wings were itching something rotten. As long as I just go on the big wheel, he thought, and stay in my seat, it isn't the same thing as flying. In fact I doubt if you could say that the two activities were in any way related.

'Two tickets, please,' said Buster to the lady in the booth who was taking the money for the ride.

'Two? Who's going with you, then?' she asked.

'Me, and me again,' said Buster.

It was just as he was about to climb into the gondola that would take him up to the glorious heights above Puddliepool-on-Sea that he heard someone calling for help. Buster stopped.

'Well, Sonny Jim, are you going on the ride or not?' said the man who operated the big wheel.

'Yes,' said Buster.

Buddleia. There it was again. A very high-pitched sound indeed.

Buster sighed.

'No,' he said.

It was a sound that no fairy can ignore. It was the sound of another fairy in big trouble.

Chapter Eleven

'Make up your mind,' said the big wheel operator. 'Are you coming or are you going?'

But Buster was now well down the wooden-slatted pier, heading towards the source of the sound. It seemed to be coming from inside a fortune-teller's booth. Buster pushed the door. It wasn't locked and it swung open. The booth was dark, but in the light from the doorway he was able to see two figures. One was large and wearing a day-glo vest, the other was a wiry fellow holding a mallet. Red light flickered in the fragments of glass that lay scattered on the floor. Under the table, her wing shining, crouched a terrified-looking lady. She was stuffing broken pieces of glass into her handbag.

Buster didn't waste a moment. He knew a fairy when he saw one. He pushed past the two thugs and grabbed her by the hand.

'Let's get out of here,' he said.

'Don't mind if I do,' said the lady.

'Buster Ignatius Spicer, at your service,' said Buster as they sprinted down the pier. 'What's your name?'

'E . . . E . . . Edie . . . Eeee, love, I'm so out of breath. I don't think I can run any more.'

They had just reached the big wheel when Buster looked back to see that the two villains were hard on their heels. Edie, he could tell, was in no state to go any farther. He had to do something or they would both end up like the crystal ball – in pieces.

'I'll go on the ride now,' he said to the big wheel operator.

'Are you sure?' said the operator. 'You don't want to think about it a bit longer?'

'I have two tickets,' said Buster as he and Edie climbed into the gondola. The operator closed the little door.

'Hey, you!' shouted the thug wearing the day-glo vest. 'Wait – I want to go in that one too.'

'You can't,' said the operator. '

You have to buy a ticket first.'

At that moment, to Buster's relief, the gondola started to rock, and rose slowly into the cloudless sky. The higher Buster and Edie went, the smaller the thugs became, but Buster knew they would be waiting to pounce the minute the big wheel returned them to earth.

'Can you fly?' asked Buster as their gondola reached its highest point.

'No, love, not with only the one wing. And I am so out of practice.'

'Buddleia,' said Buster.

The gondola reached the top of its circle and began to descend. The two villains very quickly started to look bigger again.

'We have no choice,' said Buster. 'We will have to make a flying leap.'

'Oh, love, I don't know,' said Edie. 'I mean, I haven't used my wings since . . . since Queen Victoria was a little girl.'

'Where's your fairy spirit?' said Buster, and stood up.

Suddenly, an alarm rang and the big wheel stopped turning.

'Sit down immediately,' shouted the ride operator. 'It's not safe to stand.'

'Are you ready?' asked Buster.

'As ready as I'll ever be – with one wing,' said Edie.

She took Buster's hand and they jumped out of the gondola. For one terrible moment, it seemed as if they would crash on to the pier below. Buster did his best not to let go of Edie, who clung limpet-tight to her handbag. Then, after what felt like an age, Edie started to use her wing and they soared up into the air.

It was not a graceful flight but it was sensational enough that all who saw it stared, open mouthed in wonder. Buster was confident that he hadn't broken the Fairy Code. You were allowed to break every rule in the book if another fairy was in trouble.

They landed at – or rather flew smack into – the tram stop across from the promenade.

'Oh no, look,' said Edie

A crowd of people were rushing off South Pier, pointing

at Buster and Edie. Among them Buster glimpsed an orange day-glo vest. They were still being followed. Just then, a tram whizzed to a halt and he and Edie jumped aboard.

'Fares, passes, excuses,' shouted the conductor.

'Excuses,' said Buster.

'What excuse do you have?' said the conductor.

'We're both fairies,' said Buster.

The conductor nearly fell down laughing.

'I've had a few but never one as good as that,' he said.

'Here . . .' said Edie, rummaging in her handbag. 'Here's my bus pass and the lad's fare.'

'Are you going in for the talent contest, then? You'll be needing another wing if your act is to TAKE OFF!'

The conductor laughed like a drain at his own joke.

Buster had turned to look out of the window. On the promenade the two villains were fast disappearing in the distance as they failed to catch up with the tram. Buster grinned to himself. This is more like it, he thought. This is a proper investigation.

'So, Edie,' he said. 'What's this all about, then?'

Chapter Twelve

Mr Trickett looked worn out, the shine of his permanent smile wearing thin. He wasn't having a good day – in that, Blinky Belvale had been right.

The bank manager had just phoned to say that no further loans would be forthcoming while the Johnny Carmichael murder was being investigated. Mr Trickett was beginning to wonder how much longer he could stay in business. But over his dead body would he sell his beloved ballroom to Blinky Belvale. If that wasn't gloomy enough, there was now this problem with Theo Callous, the presenter of The Me Moment.

The Me Moment was a talent contest that was to be filmed in the Starburst Ballroom. It had been quite a feather in Mr Trickett's cap to have persuaded the producers to put on the show in his ballroom. He had guaranteed them he would find some class acts. And so far he hadn't. Now Theo Callous was threatening to take his show elsewhere. And with it, much-needed income.

So far Mr Trickett's scouts had only managed to come up with a three-legged dancing dog with a one-legged owner, and a girl who could balance on a ball while holding her pet hamster. And a boy with a singing fish.

'They're not going to rock the world, are they?' said Theo Callous to Mr Trickett. 'Honestly, I expected better. Is that really all you can drag up from the murky depths of this place? You promised me a spectacle, and I have come all this way for what?'

'I do have wonderful dancers,' said Mr Trickett. 'Shall I show you some videos?'

But Theo wasn't listening. He was studying his handsome features in the dressing-room mirror. Straight nose, sculptured lips, a cliff of a jutting jaw, thick golden hair, skin the colour of burnished bronze and just as shiny. His face possessed only two expressions: one, pleased with a dazzling white smile; the second, cross without the dazzling white smile. All others had been lost

under a cosmetic surgeon's knife.

'What I need is a bit of sparkle, jazz, razzmatazz,' said Theo Callous, tearing himself away from the mirror. 'A three-legged dancing dog is not exactly The Me Moment I'm looking for. Neither, for that matter, is a murder.'

'No,' said Mr Trickett, feeling rather hot under the collar. 'It's most unfortunate about Johnny Carmichael.'

'You can say that again. A murderer on the loose. No one will turn up to see *me* if they think they might be killed while watching the show. Upsetting is a word that does little to describe the way I am feeling right now. I turned down Las Vegas to come to this dump.'

'It will be all right on the night, trust me,' said Mr Trickett. 'The murderer will be found soon. Puddliepool police are on it.'

'If they are anything like your talent scouts then I won't hold my breath,' said Theo, adding more bronze dust to his sparkling face. He stopped to answer his mobile phone.

'Yeah,' he said. 'Yeah. Yeah. Yeah, they sound more like it. Quite honestly I would listen to a singing horse if it was any good, I am that desperate. Bring them here – let me see for myself.' He turned to Mr Trickett. 'Seems one of your talent scouts spotted a giant girl and a man in a cat costume. Now that's the kind of tinsel we're looking for. That has more of a Me Moment feel to it. I'll need Morris to play the Wurlitzer.'

'That's a problem,' said Mr Trickett, and felt like adding, one of many. 'Morris has vanished.'

Explaining that Morris was wanted by the police for questioning wasn't easy. But luckily, any conversation that didn't have Theo Callous's name at the beginning, middle or end wasn't a conversation in which Theo Callous had much interest.

He interrupted Mr Trickett.

'Tell me – what's The Me Moment catchphrase?' he said.

Mr Trickett said quickly, 'ME, ME, what about ME? It's ME that matters most.'

'*Exactament*. Close the door behind you.'

Mr Trickett went to leave. As he opened the dressing-room door a song drifted down the corridor.

'Hold on, what's that?' said Theo Callous.

When he and Theo reached the ballroom, Mr Trickett couldn't believe his eyes. There stood the tallest little girl either of them had ever seen. She had fair, plaited hair and dimples, and looked as sweet as an iced cupcake. A giant iced cupcake. And as for the man she was with, his cat costume was most realistic, and over it he was wearing a cream linen suit and a straw boater hat. He carried several buckets and spades.

'Are you for real?' Theo Callous said, tugging at Fidget's fur.

Fidget straightened his jacket and looked none too pleased at having his fur pulled the wrong way.

'I have, if you must know, a medical condition,' he said.

'Purrrr,' said Theo Callous. 'Just purrfect. 'Now, sweetheart, what's your name?' he said, looking up at Primrose. Her height alone was enough to guarantee a TV audience numbering in the millions.

'Primrose.'

'Beautiful. Well, flower, what can you do?'

'Sing,' said Primrose.

And she did, her voice filling the Starburst Ballroom – with ratings gold as far as Theo Callous was concerned.

'That is the voice of an angel!' he cried, throwing his arms in the air.

Primrose giggled.

'That's what Daddy calls me.'

Chapter Thirteen

This, Emily decided, was perhaps the stupidest thing they had ever done. She'd had a feeling all along that building sandcastles on the beach with a giant's daughter and a man-sized cat wasn't the best of ideas. And then Primrose had started to sing. Almost straightaway a crowd of people had gathered round them. At first it had been a relief to be saved by the talent scout, but now some silly presenter was talking about making Primrose a star. The last thing they needed to do was draw attention to themselves. Emily walked on to the dance floor.

'Excuse me,' she said to Theo Callous. 'We have to leave.'

'Spot on the fishcake,' said Fidget.

'No-no-NO!' said Theo Callous. 'Not so fast.' He looked down at Emily and Doughnut. 'You go, by all means. And that shark on four legs.'

'He's a miniature dachshund,' said Emily. 'Come along, Primrose.'

She took Primrose's hand.

'I don't want to leave,' said Primrose. 'I want to stay here and sing. I feel happy when I sing.'

'You can sing at Wings & Co,' said Emily.

'I like this place,' Primrose said. 'It's so shiny and pretty and it's the right size for me.'

'There – that settles it. Primrose and the cat stay. Don't let me keep you,' said Theo Callous, pushing Emily towards the door. Doughnut barked at him wildly. 'Dogs aren't allowed in here.'

'But . . .' said Emily.

'And I can see,' said Theo Callous, 'that you have no talent whatsoever.'

And before Emily could say another word she and Doughnut found themselves in the foyer outside the ballroom.

'Goodbye, dearie,' called Theo Callous.

Emily was not going to be put down so easily by a man who looked like a sparkly orange. She stood in the foyer wondering what to do. She felt sure that Fidget would untangle himself and Primrose before too long. Should she wait or should she go? It was Doughnut who made the decision. A sign by the stairs said 'To the Gallery', and Doughnut ran up them, ears flapping. Emily called him back but it was hopeless. There was nothing to do but follow.

The stairs led to an empty, unlit balcony above the ballroom. Below she could see Primrose and Fidget on the dance floor.

'Doughnut,' called Emily quietly into the darkness. Where was that dog? 'Doughnut, come back here. What are you doing?'

But Doughnut didn't appear.

'Oh dear,' said Emily to herself. 'Now what?'

Suddenly she glimpsed a shadowy figure behind a pillar. In the darkness glittered a fairy wing.

'Hello,' she whispered. 'I'm Emily Vole from Wings & Co. Who are you?'

A voice from the dark said, 'Wings & Co? Oh, thank goodness! Please help me.'

'You could start by telling me your name,' said Emily.

'I'm Morris Flipwinkle.'

'Morris Flipwinkle? You . . . you . . . you're wanted by the police for the murder of Johnny Carmichael,' said Emily. She wondered if she shouldn't make a run for the nearest phone box and call James.

'Yes,' said Morris. 'But I didn't do it. Please believe me . . . I'm innocent. I wouldn't hurt a wombat.'

He emerged from the shadows carrying Doughnut. There was no doubt that he was in a sorry state, all crumpled and tired looking. He wasn't the least bit threatening and Emily couldn't help feeling sorry for him. She made a snap decision. She would take him back to Wings & Co for questioning. But, oh dear – how? She couldn't very well just walk out of the Starburst Ballroom and down the promenade in broad daylight with the most wanted man in Puddliepool-on-Sea.

'Stay here,' said Emily to Morris. 'I'm going to see if I can find a disguise for you.'

'Like what?' asked Morris, clinging to Doughnut as if his freedom depended on him. 'Crikey, don't be long.'

Emily wasn't sure what she was looking for. There must, she supposed, be a cupboard with cleaning things in it, and if there was such a cupboard, there might be an overall or a scarf or something inside.

But when she found the cupboard, all she could see was a black bin bag stuffed in the corner. She was about to close the cupboard when she saw something white poking out of the bag. It was a curly wig. Quickly she pulled it out, and then a colourful scarf, a pair of sunglasses, a fluffy coat and some horrible, ugly shoes. Emily gathered up everything and went back to where she had left Morris and Doughnut.

'Put these on,' she said to Morris.

'Crikey,' said Morris again. 'They must have belonged to someone's granny.'

Emily helped Morris put on the wig and hat. He tied the scarf round his neck and buttoned up the coat. At Emily's suggestion, he rolled up his trousers, revealing his skinny legs. Finally, he put on the shoes, amazed to find that they fitted.

'All I can say is, with shoes this big, she must have been a very large granny,' said Morris.

A voice called from the landing below.

'Hello – who's up there?'

'Crikey crickets,' said Morris. 'I've been caught. It's all over.'

'Don't panic,' said Emily. 'Here – put on the dark glasses and start acting as if you're my grandma.'

A security man came panting and puffing up the stairs.

'You shouldn't be here, little girl,' he said.

Thinking quickly, Emily explained that Granny had been desperate for the toilet and they had become somewhat lost. Morris kept his head down and did his best to hide his unshaven chin in the scarf. Doughnut put on his most lost expression.

'We have a granny and her granddaughter up here,' said the security guard into his walkie-talkie. 'The old lady is a bit wobbly on her pins. Over.' He listened to the voice crackling on the other end and then said, 'Roger. I'll send them out by the nearest exit.' He turned to Emily. 'Just go down the stairs and keep going until you reach the ground floor. And please hold on to the handrail – for Health & Safety.'

Chapter Fourteen

uster arrived back at Wings & Co with Edie, both of them flushed and out of breath. Buster had constantly checked that no one was following them on the way there. All he had seen on the promenade outside the shop was an odd-looking seagull eating scraps of fish and chips in the gutter. It had the strangest bulgy eyes. Buster felt pretty sure seagulls weren't meant to look like that. It was only when he was inside Wings & Co with the front door closed behind them that he felt safe.

Edie didn't. The sight of the magic lamp was enough to worry any fairy. She edged away from it. That lamp didn't have a good history, that was for sure.

'We're all doomed,' said the lamp. 'Doomed, I tell you.'

'Yes, but where is everybody?' asked Buster.

'Don't ask me. I'm a nobody around here,' replied the

magic lamp. 'You all went off to the beach – hours ago – leaving me to look after the sick keys. We're doomed, I tell you.'

'Oh, put a cork in it,' said Buster.

'Eee, love, I feel a bit faint,' said Edie.

Buster helped her to a chair and Edie sat there looking miserable.

'Are you sure that lamp isn't going to do anything nasty?'

'Don't worry,' said Buster. 'It did once work for the wicked witch Harpella, but since Emily Vole took out the dragon's tooth it's turned over a new leaf. As for Harpella, she's now a purple rabbit and long may she stay that way.'

'I heard about that. Still, it's hard to believe the lamp's harmless,' said Edie, 'when you think of all the damage it's done.'

'It wasn't my fault, don't go blaming me,' said the magic lamp. 'It was all Harpella's doing.' It flounced up the stairs.

'What's gone wrong?' said Edie sadly. 'I should have seen all this coming. I mean, I see most things in my crystal ball. I should have known what was going to happen to Morris Flipwinkle. After all, he came and asked me what his future held. As for getting my wings back, that would have been like looking into a window. It's almost as if I've been foggled.'

Buster looked up, sharply. 'What did you see?' he asked.

'That's the trouble, love. I couldn't make head nor tail of it. Each picture I saw seemed to come from a different story.'

'I don't understand,' said Buster.

'Neither do I,' said Edie, opening her handbag. 'Here, love, have a look for yourself. I gathered up three pieces of my crystal ball while those hooligans were wrecking my booth. The images are frozen on them.' She handed the large fragments of glass to Buster. He took them carefully to the light to study. In one piece he saw a skeleton, in another he saw a diamond and, in the third, a seagull. 'The only thing I can think of is that the diamond is connected to that robbery in London.'

'The skeleton looks like something out of a ghost train. But maybe it's to do with the murder,' said Buster.

But before Edie could answer the doorbell rang.

'Oh no,' she said. 'They've found us.'

The lamp came bustling down the stairs.

'What is wrong with you? There's someone wanting to come in. Am I expected to do everything around here?'

'Wait,' said Buster. 'Let me check who it is.'

Buster went to the door. He was relieved to see that the two thugs hadn't found them. It was Emily and Doughnut, although with them was an old woman he didn't recognise.

'Where are Fidget and Primrose?' asked Buster as he let them in, checking the street in both directions again as he did so.

Emily explained about the talent contest and how Fidget and Primrose had come to be at the Starburst Ballroom.

'And that was when I found . . .' She stopped and looked at Edie. 'Excuse me . . . Buster, are you going to introduce me to this lady?'

'Oh, this is Edie Girdle, a fairy with one wing,' said Buster.

'A pleasure to meet you,' said Edie.

'And are you going introduce me to this lady?' said Buster.

'It's not a lady,' said Emily.

Morris took off the wig and stood there looking foolish.

'Morris Flipwinkle! Well, blow my socks off,' said Edie.

'Emily – he's wanted in connection with a murder!' said Buster. 'You should have told the police, not brought him here. We're a fairy detective agency. We aren't involved in that case.'

'I think we might be,' said Emily.

'How so?' asked Buster.

'Doomed! We're all doomed,' cried the magic lamp.

'Take off the coat, Morris,' said Emily.

Morris did as he was told and unfolded his wing.

'Buddleia,' said Buster. 'But just because he's a fairy doesn't mean he didn't kill Johnny Carmichael.'

'That's why I brought him here for questioning,' said Emily. She was somewhat put out by Buster's reaction. He would have been so pleased with himself if he'd brought a suspected murderer in for questioning. 'Anyway, I don't think he is the murderer.'

'Hold on a mo,' said Edie. 'Let's see if I still have any of my magic powers left. Morris, give me your hand, love.'

Edie Girdle studied Morris's palm. Emily's eyes widened as something amazing happened. Edie Girdle seemed to light up from inside, and, glowing, she slowly she rose from her chair before clattering down with a bang.

'Well, that sorted that out,' she said. 'I'm glad to know I haven't lost all my talents.'

'What did you see?' asked Emily.

'That Morris definitely didn't kill Johnny Carmichael.'

'How can you be sure?'

'It isn't in his nature or in the palm of his hand,' said Edie.

'Did you see who the murderer was?'

'Unfortunately, I didn't, love. I wish I had.' Edie smiled at Morris. 'I always thought you might be a fairy but I wasn't sure.'

'I just wish that I had both my wings,' said Morris. 'Then I would fly away from all this mess.'

'Doomed, I tell you, doomed!' said the lamp.

Emily turned to the lamp.

'Would you please make some tea for our guests?'

'Run here, run there, run, run. Am I no more than a servant?'

'You are not a servant,' said Emily firmly. 'But can't you see we have a lot on? I would have thought 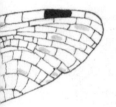 that a lamp of your brainage would have worked that out by now. But no, all we have had from you is a pantomime of dramas.'

'Oh, sweet mistress, forgive me! I didn't mean . . .'

'Tea,' said Emily. 'And not another word from your spout.'

Chapter Fifteen

Cheryl Spike was a bit confused. She had no idea where her boss, Blinky Belvale, had gone. When she and The Toad had returned from their fruitless search for the fortune-teller, he had been sitting at his desk. A few minutes later she'd poked her head into his office and he wasn't there. The window was open but the office was on the second floor. He couldn't have gone out that way.

'It's not natural,' she said to The Toad. 'It gives me the creeps.'

The Toad was pacing up and down.

'We should call it a day,' he said, blowing a huge bubble from his mouth rather than popping it.

'No. Not yet,' replied Cheryl. 'You need to stay calm.' She pulled a plan of the Starburst Ballroom out of her day-glo jacket. 'Where've you looked so far?'

The Toad stared at the plan.

'I told you. Blooming everywhere under the stage.'

'Then maybe,' said Cheryl, 'we need to look in the ghost train.'

'I'm not going down there. It's spooky. And that new waxwork scares me rotten,' said The Toad. 'Anyway, it's not safe. Not with the Old Bill snooping around.'

He popped a huge bubble.

'CHERYL!' bellowed the unmistakable voice of Blinky Belvale, making them both jump out of their skins.

Cheryl and The Toad looked at each other nervously. Cheryl opened Blinky Belvale's office door. Her boss was sitting behind his desk, eating fish and chips out of newspaper. Where had he come from?

'Didn't see you come in, Mr B,' said Cheryl. 'Never saw you go out either.'

Blinky looked up at her, his eyes bulging from his head.

'Did you do what I asked?' he said, stuffing yet more chips into his mouth.

'Yes, Mr B.'

'No you didn't,' said Blinky, spitting out bits of food.

'You let the flying boy and the dancing fortune-teller escape.'

How he knew that, Cheryl had no idea. She was beginning to think that her boss had eyes in the back of that pork-pie hat of his.

'Do I have to do everything round here?' he said. 'I give you a simple task and what you do? You bungle it.'

'You only told us to smash the crystal ball. You didn't say anything about the old girl with the one wing. Or a flying boy.'

Blinky stood up.

'Are you telling me that the dancing fortune-teller has a wing?'

'Ye-eah,' said Cheryl uncertainly. She was not given to much imagination, and for a moment she wondered if she'd been right about the wing.

Blinky pushed back his chair.

'Another unwanted can of worms,' he muttered to himself. 'An infestation of interfering fairies.'

'Sorry, Mr B – what did you say?' said Cheryl.

She noticed there was a feather on the carpet and what

looked like bird droppings. She was about to ask if a bird had flown in through the window when she caught the look on Blinky Belvale's face. It was a look that made her think twice.

'Has Trickett found any talent for his contest yet?' asked Blinky.

'Don't know,' said Cheryl.

'Find out. Give them a call,' said Blinky.

Cheryl padded back to her desk and picked up the phone.

'Yeah. Nah. Yeah,' she said and hung up.

'What's going on?' asked Blinky.

'They're auditioning a man in a cat costume and a giant little girl who can sing,' said Cheryl, reading from her notes.

Blinky Belvale only knew of one man-sized cat and he didn't like what he knew.

'Come on,' he said.

Cheryl followed her boss out of his office, down the stairs and on to the promenade.

'Where're we going?' she asked.

'Where do you think?' said Blinky.

'I try not to, Mr B,' replied Cheryl.

'The Starburst Ballroom,' growled Blinky Belvale.

The security guard working for The Me Moment tried to stop Blinky Belvale and his personal assistant from entering.

'Auditions are in progress,' he said.

'The boss needs to have another look at the ballroom,' said Cheryl, as the boss pushed past the security guard.

Before anyone could stop them, Blinky Belvale and Cheryl muscled their way on to the dance floor. A giant girl was singing about rose bushes.

'Well, well,' muttered Blinky to himself, 'look who it is.'

Then, under the gallery, sitting at a table, Blinky saw Fidget the cat.

'Cheryl, I don't trust that cat. Phone The Toad and tell him to get down to the ghost train and keep an eye on my waxwork.'

'Now, Mr B?'

'Yes-of-course-now. I'm going to see what Trickett is up to.'

Chapter Sixteen

'B ut a minute ago you said Johnny Carmichael's murder had nothing to do with Wings & Co,' said Emily to Buster as he buttered the toast.

The magic lamp poured boiling water into a complaining teapot.

'I've changed my mind,' replied Buster. 'I'm beginning to think this is one of the most interesting cases we've had in a long time.' Emily followed him as he carried the tea tray upstairs. 'You wouldn't understand, seeing you are a girl and new to the business of being a detective.'

Emily wondered – as she often did – whoever had thought up boys, for they hadn't done a very good job. She opened the door to the drawing room, glad to find that it was still where it had been last time. The curtains blew gently in the sea breeze. Edie was seated on the green velvet sofa. Next to her perched Morris.

Morris wasn't very good at sitting still. He looked twitchy, and even the tea and toast didn't do all that much to anchor him to the furniture.

Buster pulled up a chair and took out his notebook.

'Best,' he said, 'that you start at the beginning.'

And Morris did.

It was a rather long beginning, and by the time Morris Flipwinkle had reached the middle, Emily's mind had wandered to another problem. What on earth was keeping Fidget and Primrose? Fidget could usually be relied upon to escape from any sticky situation.

Emily stared absent-mindedly at what Buster had written in his notebook:

Pink jumper.

One wing.

Face an unopened Christmas present.

Then he had doodled a picture of a roller coaster, and beside that was a rather good drawing of an odd-looking seagull. Below it, he had written the word

DIAMOND surrounded by wiggly lines.

Why diamond? wondered Emily.

'Was there anything unusual about that afternoon?'
Buster asked Morris.

'Yes,' interrupted Edie, who had been listening to all
this. 'The Wurlitzer was out of tune.'

'The C note was a bit flat,' said Morris. 'And I thought
once I'd finished my set, I would see what was wrong with
the old girl.'

'Old girl?' asked Emily.

'The Wurlitzer,' Morris explained. 'That's what I call
her.'

'Oh,' said Emily.

'But you didn't, did you?' said Buster.

'I didn't what?' asked Morris.

'You didn't have a chance to look inside the Wurlitzer.'

'No,' said Morris. 'The minute the Wurlitzer and I
arrived below stage, there was Johnny Carmichael, prowling
back and forth like an over-boiled tiger. I asked him what
was wrong and he told me to push off if I knew what was
good for me.'

'Wow,' said Emily. 'That was rude of him. Did he often talk to you like that?'

'Yes,' replied Morris. 'He never liked me much.'

'I suppose,' said Emily, 'that might be thought reason enough for you to bump him off.'

'But I didn't,' said Morris. 'I wouldn't.'

'No, love, you couldn't,' echoed Edie.

'So you left,' said Buster, ignoring Morris's outcry. 'And then you remembered that you'd forgotten to tell him that the C was flat?'

'Yes,' said Morris. 'I ran back.'

'How long before you returned?' asked Emily.

Timing, she had read, was important in an investigation. Though to be honest, fairies and clocks never really worked that well together. Fairies, she had learned through experience, tended to live in their own time, which was quite different from humans'.

'A matter of moments,' said Morris. 'It was dark under the stage with only one work light. I saw Johnny sitting at the Wurlitzer bolt upright, still as a statue. I didn't see the knife, not until I was much closer, on account of his dinner jacket. And even then I thought it was a joke. I mean, Johnny liked to play tricks on me, to make me look a fool. I was used to them.'

'So you believed that he was pretending to be dead?' said Buster. 'Until you touched the knife?'

'I didn't know that he was really dead. Honestly, I thought he was just messing about. Then I got frightened. What was I to do? My fingerprints were all over the murder weapon.'

Edie patted Morris's hand.

'There, there, love,' she said. 'You weren't to know.'

'What happened then?' asked Emily.

'One moment I had my hand on the knife then everything went into a terrible whirl. Time stood still and, then, there I was, in front of the curious cabinet. The key turned in the lock and I found that only one of my glorious wings had been returned to me. I ran away and hid in the one place the police would least expect to find me, the Starburst Ballroom.'

'You didn't see the murderer?' said Emily.

'I did and I didn't. I saw his shoes,' said Morris.

'Hopeless,' muttered Emily to herself.

'You saw the shoes because they were the only things that showed up in the darkness down there?' said Buster suddenly. 'The heels flashed with red lights, didn't they?'

'Yes,' said Morris miserably. 'How did you know?'

Buster shrugged and in that moment Emily realised to her great annoyance that he was keeping something from her. As usual.

'Then he and his shoes disappeared through the door leading to the ghost train,' said Morris.

'Interesting,' said Buster. 'Very interesting indeed. And the ghost train runs under the ballroom, you say?'

Morris nodded.

Buster stood up.

'Come on, Emily. We need to visit the scene of the crime, talk to people who were there. There's work to be done.'

'Yes,' said Emily. 'For a start you might tell me what it is you know that I don't and stop being vain, arrogant, unreasonable and difficult to work with. In short, behaving like a prima donna.'

'A what?' said Buster.

'You heard,' said Emily.

Buster looked a little stunned.

'OK. Sorry,' he said. 'I worked on my own for a hundred years and I'm not used to being part of a team. I have a hunch and I'll tell you about it on the way to the Starburst Ballroom.'

'I have a hunch too,' said Emily. 'Fidget said the shop brought us to Puddliepool-on-Sea for a reason. I'm beginning to think that the reason might be that Billy Buckle is here.'

Chapter Seventeen

If it hadn't been for the fact that Primrose was so happy, Fidget would have left the Starburst Ballroom hours ago. He didn't like Theo Callous and his Me Moment show one little bit. There were too many 'me moments' in the lives of human beings already and all of them, as far as Fidget could see, ended in trouble. Fidget just wanted to go home. He needed a catnap. A day without naps and fishpaste sandwiches was a day when something wasn't right in the trawling net of life.

He had seated himself away from the dance floor, at one of the round tables under the pillars that held up the gallery above. Theo Callous had forgotten him, which was good, for it gave Fidget a chance to properly look about. It was then he noticed that every so often the ballroom shook. Having once been a master builder, Fidget knew a thing or two about bricks and mortar. He knew there was little cause for a building to wobble unless an earthquake or a landslide or something was wobbling it. So what was it?

Primrose's voice rose high into the painted ceiling of the ballroom, where cherubs, princes and princesses beamed down on her.

Somewhere over the rose bush
Skies are blue
Somewhere over that rose bush
I will wait for you.

By now even Theo Callous, who usually noticed very little except his own reflection, had commented on the shaky ballroom floor.

Curiosity was what made Fidget a great detective. Curiosity was what had led to him to only having eight of his nine lives left. Curiosity was what made him now take off his shoes so that he could prowl about in the murky darkness under the gallery until he found a door marked 'Staff Only'. That door interested him.

Cats have claws for good reasons, and Fidget's had proved most useful over the centuries, especially with locked doors. It only took a jigger and a jag for the door to give way. Fidget checked that no one was watching him. Fortunately all eyes were on Primrose. She sang:

I used to dream upon a star
Now I know they're very far
Lost among a sparkling sea
Will you ever fi-ind me?

Again the ballroom shook.

On velvet paws, Fidget slipped through the door and down some steps.

He would never say so, for it would be boasting – and that was a thing Fidget never did – but really a cat makes the most perfect detective. Not only has a cat clever claws and silent paws, he also has eyes that can see in the dark.

He found himself standing in a tunnel beside some tracks. Rattling towards him, the noise of it peppered with screams and echoing electronic laughter, was a small, brightly painted open car.

Mash my mushy peas, thought Fidget, as it hurtled down the tracks. So this is what's causing all the noise and shaking. He shook his head sadly. Who would do such a terrible thing to such a lovely building?

The front of the car was the shape of a monster's head, its mouth wide open. Inside, sitting bold upright, was a terrified dad with his son, who appeared less terrified – that is, until the boy suddenly saw a man-sized cat lit up by the whirling lights.

The boy let out an ear-piercing scream.

'DAD! Look – it's enormous!'

The moment the carriage had gone, Fidget scampered across the tracks to where skeletons loomed, their eyes bobbing out of their skulls, and then through into the next chamber. Corpses bicycled round and round him, lit by flashing neon. He caught a glimpse of a huge cage in the chamber beyond. It was guarded by two flapping doors.

Fidget's fur began to bristle, which told him straightaway that something decidedly fishy – something that needed investigation – was going on beyond the flapping doors. They only opened when one of the painted cars banged through them. There was nothing for it but to hitch a ride. Fidget waited. He chose a carriage carrying

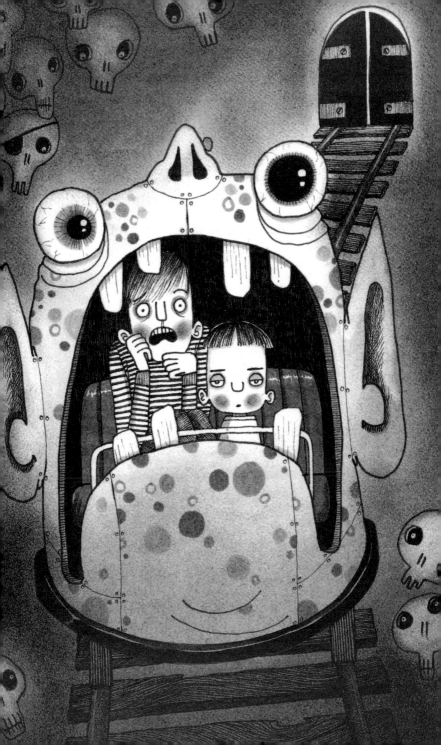

two lads. Above the noise, Fidget heard one boast to the other.

'You think this is scary? It's pants.'

'Yeah,' said his friend. 'This is a ghost train for babies.'

Fidget sprang on to the back of their car. When the two lads turned and came face to face with a giant cat, they let out shrieks worthy of any horror movie.

Once through the doors, Fidget jumped off the car, grinning. Now he was in a vaulted chamber, larger and taller than the others. It was filled with mist and cobwebs, and in the middle stood a ginormous cage. In it, Fidget could just make out two huge legs ending in two huge red shoes. Mayonnaise my tuna, he said to himself. It can't possibly be . . . how would he have got down here? It must be a waxwork.

Above him, Primrose started to sing again.

Somewhere over the rose bush . . .

A groan rumbled round the chamber, shaking the vaulted ceiling. Fidget was about to investigate further when he realised he was not alone. Through the mist he saw the shadowy figure of a man and, creeping along the floor, two flashing red lights.

Fidget looked around. There was nowhere for a man-sized cat to hide. Time to get out of here – and fast. But tomorrow he'd be back to take a closer look at that waxwork.

Chapter Eighteen

The walls of Mr Trickett's office were covered with peeling posters of dancers from the past. The manager's desk was piled high with papers, a half-eaten pizza, and a lot of worrying brown envelopes. It didn't take a fairy detective to work out that things were not looking good for the business, thought Emily.

Mr Trickett paced up and down.

'I have enough on my plate,' he said, 'without you two kids causing trouble. How on earth did you get past the security guards?'

It was a good question and Emily doubted if Mr Trickett would really want to know the answer. Buster had flown up, holding tight to Emily, until they had reached the top floor, where they had climbed in through the toilet window.

'I know what your game is, young lady,' said Mr Trickett to Emily. 'You're trying to sneak your way on to The Me Moment. Mr Callous has already told you . . .'

'No,' said Emily. 'We're worried about our two friends.'

She saw that Buster was trying to read the papers on the desk upside down and nudged him. 'Aren't we, Buster?'

'Yes. Mr Fidget and a little girl called Primrose,' said Buster.

They had agreed that this would be a good way to start the interview with Mr Trickett.

'You mean that ginormous girl with plaits and the man in the cat costume?'

'We do,' said Emily.

'Well, the cat failed the audition. Pity. It's one of the best costumes I've ever seen. But no other talent apart from saying "spot on the fishcake" and knitting. The girl, on the other hand, is something special. I don't need a crystal ball to see that she is going to be a star. Forgive the pun – a giant career is waiting for her.'

'Hold on a mo,' said Buster. 'She's only six years old.'

'Six?' repeated Mr Trickett. 'Impossible. She's well over two metres tall. All that little kiddie thing is an act, isn't it?'

'No,' said Emily firmly. 'She's six and needs her father's consent before she can appear on any show.'

'All right, all right. I need this show to be a success,' said Mr Trickett, tapping his fingers on the desk. 'That shouldn't be too difficult. Where's her father?'

'Mr Buckle is missing,' said Emily. 'That's what we're investigating.'

'Investigating?'

'Yes,' said Emily, handing him a business card on which was printed:

Wings & Co.

Fairy Detective Agency

'What are you two, a couple of comedians?'

'No, we are detectives,' said Buster. 'And we also have a client with an interest in the murder of Johnny Carmichael.'

Mr Trickett's face collapsed into folds of anxiety. He stared, bewildered, at Buster and Emily.

'Look. I have enough problems right now, like the murder and Blinky Belvale for starters. Primrose can't be six, that's impossible. Now, you two clowns, scarper.'

'She is six,' said Emily. 'Without parental consent, you'll be in even more trouble than you already are.'

'But if you will help us,' said Buster, 'we'll try to help you.'

Mr Trickett slumped in his chair, defeated.

'Five minutes,' said Buster. 'That's all it will take.'

Mr Trickett glanced at his watch.

'Five minutes. Then I want you both out of here. No more games. Deal?'

'Deal. Who is Blinky Belvale?' asked Buster.

'He's the bigwig who owns the whole of the Starburst Amusement Park, except for the ballroom. And I tell you this for a stick of candyfloss, I am not selling it. My great-great-grandfather built the ballroom, and this is where my heart belongs. Murder or no murder, Blinky Belvale will not lay his slimy hands on my son's inheritance.'

'What's the murder got to do with your son's inheritance?' asked Emily.

'Well, the bank's not going to lend me another penny until this mess is cleared up. In other words, I'm up duck alley. This is just what Belvale has been waiting for.'

Emily took out her notebook and wrote in large letters BLINKY BELVALE. A strange name, she thought. Like a made-up name.

'Mr Trickett,' she said. 'Is it possible that Blinky Belvale murdered Johnny Carmichael? After all, he seems to have a motive.'

A mouse poked its head out from behind a filing cabinet and started to eat a scrap of pizza that had fallen to the floor.

'I wouldn't put anything past that man,' said Mr Trickett.

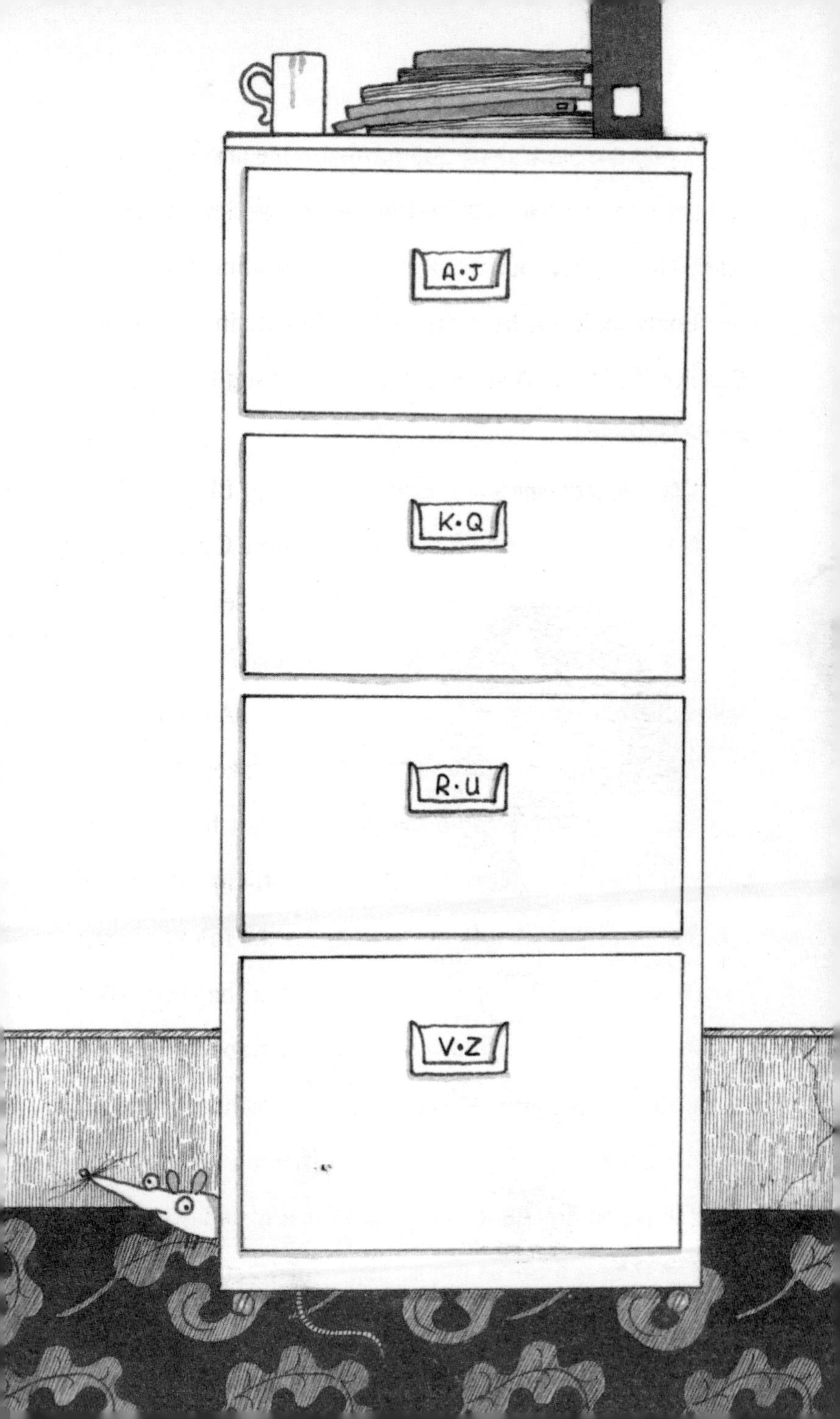
A·J
K·Q
R·U
V·Z

'What did you do when you discovered that Mr Carmichael was dead?' asked Buster.

'I called the police. What else would I do? Then I went upstairs to the ballroom and I was told that Edie Girdle had vanished. I sent one of my staff to check the toilets in case she was locked in. It happens, you know.'

'Yes,' said Emily. 'But she wasn't.'

'No, she wasn't,' said Mr Trickett. 'And now Morris Flipwinkle has vanished too.'

'The ghost train runs under the dance floor,' said Buster. 'Is that right?'

'Yes,' said Mr Trickett. 'Mr Belvale told me if I made a fuss about him expanding the ride he would have my ballroom closed down on the grounds of Health & Safety.'

The mouse seemed to be listening with interest to the conversation.

Mr Trickett took off his glasses and rubbed his eyes. He stood up and stamped his foot at the mouse.

'Blasted mice,' he said, as it scuttled away.

'Tell me more about Blinky Belvale,' said Emily.

'The man is a rotten onion. There are many layers to

him and all of them smelly. You never know when he is going to turn up. Sly, that's what he is.'

'How big is the space under the ballroom?' asked Buster.

'What's that got to do with anything?'

'Just wondered,' said Buster.

Mr Trickett sighed.

'It's vast, a cavern of a place.'

'Did Mr Belvale do a lot of building work?'

'At first, but then he stopped. Then he started again about two weeks ago. Improvements, he said. Goodness knows what he was up to down there. I heard he took a donkey in one evening. I haven't a clue what that was all about.' Mr Trickett stopped. 'Look, what is the point of all these questions? No. That's enough. I have work to do. A father to find, permission to be given and a show to go on.'

'Four minutes and fifty-six seconds – so time for a last question,' said Buster.

'Come on, stop playing games,' said Mr Trickett. 'Enough is enough.' He guided them to the door.

'Did anyone see the donkey leave?' asked Buster, before the door slammed in his face.

Chapter Nineteen

Fidget managed to extract Primrose from the clutches of Theo Callous on the understanding that they would return tomorrow for rehearsals. By the time they reached Wings & Co, Fidget was exhausted. There was an unusual greyness about his tortoiseshell colouring.

'Fidget, at last you're back. I've been so worried about you,' said Emily, giving his paw a little squeeze. 'We've lots to tell you. Buster and I tried to rescue you from that awful Theo Callous but he had the security man escort us from the building.'

'Never mind, my little ducks. I have things to tell you too. I was curious about the rumble coming from under the dance floor, went down there . . . saw something . . . I'm not sure . . .' He held his tummy and looked very wobbily. 'Before I can say any more,' he said wearily,

'I need some fishpaste sandwiches and a kip.'

Primrose, on the other hand, was blooming. She appeared to have grown a little bit since breakfast, which was rather alarming, for her head now was not far from touching the ceiling. Time, Emily could see, was running out.

'I've had a most wonderful day,' Primrose told Edie as the kindly fortune-teller took her upstairs to bed. 'It's the best day I've had since Daddy's been gone.'

Soon Fidget was fast asleep in his favourite armchair, while Emily sat studying the notes she had taken when they had interviewed Mr Trickett earlier that day. The more she looked at the name Blinky Belvale the weirder it seemed to be. She sucked the end of her pencil as she looked back over the notes she had made earlier in the investigation.

The SAD DADS' BAND.

Billy Buckle played bassoon.

Hadn't played with the band for ages.

Didn't take Primrose because he had to cross the VALLEY OF DOOM where the BOG-EYED LOADER lived.

B-E.L = *Ogre, shape-shifter.*

Oh dear, thought Emily. I wish I knew what a shape-shifting ogre looked like. That's the trouble with not being a fairy.

Buster was walking back and forth like a detective in need of a deerstalker hat, or a very large magnifying glass, or both.

What he was actually thinking had nothing to do with the case. He still hadn't quite recovered from Emily's outburst. She had called him vain! Well, unlike certain people who were happy to wear knitted fish dresses, he cared about how he looked. He wasn't arrogant. Well – maybe a bit – but that was only because he knew more than anyone else. And how she could call him unreasonable, he had no idea. Perhaps she was just jealous, because he had wings and she didn't. As for difficult to work with – well, that wasn't fair. Look how patient he had been with Emily even though she wasn't a fairy – which made *her* truly difficult to work with.

'All right,' Emily said to Buster. 'Stop being mysterious and wearing a path in the carpet. What do you think?'

Buster wanted to say was that he wasn't a prima donna but his pride wouldn't let him, so instead he said, 'I think that we are dealing with a murder and an abduction.'

'Wow. What's that ab-duck word mean?' asked Emily.

'Abduction,' Buster said grandly, 'means to take someone away against their will.'

'Why didn't you say so in the first place?' said Emily. 'I suppose you mean Billy Buckle?'

'Of course. We are agreed,' said Buster, still walking back and forth, 'that in both the suspected abduction of Billy Buckle and the murder of Johnny Carmichael, the fairy world seems to be involved. So the question is, are the cases related? It's a tricky one.'

'You can say that again,' said Emily. So many bits and pieces didn't add up or even join together no matter how hard she thought about them.

'All right, then. Here's what we know, or what we think we know, or what we don't know,' said Buster. 'First of all, we think we know that the reason the shop brought us to Puddliepool-on-Sea is to help us find Billy Buckle. After all, if Primrose grows much more the old beams won't be able to take it and the shop will collapse. We know that the keys have lost their metal but we don't know why. We know that two fairies have had one wing each returned to them and we don't know why. We know that Morris Flipwinkle didn't murder Johnny Carmichael but we don't know who did. Though Blinky Belvale has a motive.'

'And we don't know,' said Emily, 'if the murder has anything to do with Billy, which takes us round in a big circle back to the beginning.'

'Not quite. We know Edie had her crystal ball smashed by two thugs. One was wearing a day-glo vest, the other wearing trainers with flashing red lights in the heels. Morris saw someone under the stage wearing trainers like those just after Johnny Carmichael was killed.'

'Perhaps they smashed the crystal ball to stop Edie seeing something in it,' said Emily. 'Like who murdered Johnny Carmichael. Oh, I don't know. Do you know, I don't think we know much at all.'

'But we do have some very important clues,' said Buster.

'You mean the fragments of Edie's crystal ball?'

'Yes,' said Buster. 'In one piece I saw a seagull . . .'

'. . . and that tells us . . . ?' asked Emily.

'Nothing except what we know already, that sea, sand and seagulls go together.

'Then there was a skeleton,' said Buster. 'Now, I have an idea about that. All over Puddliepool-on-Sea there are posters advertising a new attraction in the ghost train. Skeletons and ghost trains go together. And Fidget just said he saw something suspicious down there.'

'Or,' said Emily, 'the skeleton could just stand for a dead body, like Johnny Carmichael's, and have nothing whatsoever to do with ghost trains.'

'Last of all there was a diamond,' said Buster. 'But that doesn't fit in. The jewellery robbery happened in London, not here.'

'Still,' said Emily, 'perhaps we should tell James about it. You said he was interested in that photo of Johnny Carmichael.'

'Buddleia,' said Buster. 'I don't know.'

It was later that evening, when the sun had set in a pinkish sky, that Fidget woke up, his mind as clear as a trout stream, to find that everyone had gone to bed. Emily was tucked up with a dictionary and a large notepad.

'What are you doing, my little ducks?' asked Fidget. 'You should be asleep by now.'

Emily showed him what she had written on her notepad. It looked like a crossword puzzle and Fidget had never got the point of crossword puzzles.

He sat down at the end of the bed.

'Blinky Belvale . . .' said Emily.

'. . . is the king prawn who owns the amusement park,' said Fidget. 'That's one of the things I found out this afternoon. He turned up at the ballroom.'

'Did he?' said Emily, interested. 'I wonder why. But, anyway, Blinky means eyes in slang. It says so in this dictionary.'

'Sorry, you've caught me with a flea spray in my paw.'

'And vale is another word for valley,' said Emily. 'And that made me think of the Valley of . . .'

'. . . the piranha's pyjamas?'

'No, no, look,' said Emily, and showed him her notebook again. She had written:

B	E	L	V	A	L	E
o	y	o				
g	e	a				
	d	d				
		e				
		r				

'Nope. Haven't a flea of a clue.'

Emily started to explain. Fidget stood up.

'You're not saying what I think you're saying?'

'What do you think I am saying?' said Emily.

'That we are up a blind valley,' said Fidget.

'No!' said Emily.

Fidget twisted his whiskers.

'It's all fishpaste to me. What I think is, you need a good night's sleep. And in the morning there's a ghost train I want to take you on.'

Emily yawned.

'I would like that. Sweet dreams.'

She closed her eyes, and before you could say 'The Cat's Jim-Jams', Emily was fast asleep.

Fidget drew the curtains and turned out her bedside light. It was then that it struck him like a wet kipper on a hot day. Emily had been trying to tell him that she had made a diabolical discovery: Blinky Belvale was the Bog-Eyed Loader.

Early the following morning Detective James Cardwell was to be found sitting in his office at New Scotland Yard. He was comparing a print-out of a mugshot of the renowned diamond snatcher known as The Maestro with the photo of Johnny Carmichael that he been given by Sergeant Binns at Puddliepool Police Station. It was a black-and-white photo, and in it, Johnny was wearing an evening suit with a white bow tie. On his nose were perched large, black, round-framed glasses that hid most of his face. A moustache hid most of his mouth.

Taking up a felt-tipped pen, James purposefully drew

round-framed glasses and a moustache on the face of
The Maestro.

'Well, Maestro,' said James. 'Or should I call you
Johnny? Who killed you? And why?'

There was a knock on his door.

'Yes, come in,' said James.

The scent of roses wafted into the room and James looked up to see Poppy.

'Good morning,' she said cheerfully. 'I think you might be interested in this. Puddliepool police have had a call from a security guard who works at the Starburst Ballroom. He reported seeing a granny who matched the description of one of the women involved in the Bond Street robbery.'

'Granny?' said James. 'How does he know she's a granny?'

'Puddliepool have sent the CCTV footage,' said Poppy.

She pulled up a chair next to him and they both watched the screen.

The first camera showed a little girl creeping along a passage.

'Oh no . . .' said James faintly.

'What?' said Poppy.

'Nothing,' said James.

The second camera was on the open door of a cupboard and the little girl could be seen rummaging in a black bin bag. A few minutes later the same camera picked up a large woman in a day-glo vest who was clearly searching for something inside the cupboard.

'Who's that?' asked James.

'I don't know,' said Poppy. 'Sergeant Binns at Puddliepool might.'

The third camera was on the foyer of the ballroom.
A white-haired old lady in a scarf shuffled past. To James's
utter horror, she had Doughnut tucked under one arm and
was holding Emily by the hand.

James's stomach turned over. Emily Vole had been
abducted by a dangerous criminal.

'Poppy,' he said, 'I have to go up to Puddliepool-on-
Sea at once. Find out what you can about the woman in
the day-glo vest.'

'Will you be needing a car?' Poppy asked.

'No – I'll fly,' said James absently.

Poppy shot him a quizzical look as she left the office,
closing the door behind her.

Chapter Twenty

One of Emily's favourite things about Wings & Co was the kitchen. It always stayed put, was never given to shuffling about. Other rooms might move around but never the heart of the shop, as Fidget called the kitchen. It stayed tucked away in the basement, a cosy room with an old-fashioned stove perched on four iron legs. Above the stove on metal hooks hung the pots and pans alongside strings of onions and herbs. On the wall opposite was a huge painted sideboard filled with crotchety crockery, some dating as far back as the Georgians. There was a sink and next to it a ladder designed especially for the magic lamp so it could reach the taps. A dog basket for Doughnut was by the fireplace with seventeen little chairs for the keys to sit on and warm their boots on cold days.

A long kitchen table took up the rest of the room on top of which flowers were neatly arranged in jam jars.

Emily woke that morning to the sun shining through her curtains and the cry of the seagulls outside. She was pleased to find that they were still in Puddliepool-on-Sea and even more pleased to see James Cardwell in the kitchen, grill pan in hand and an apron over his suit, making breakfast. But James's face was very grave indeed, not full of the usual smiles and cheeriness that Emily expected. She'd never seen him looking like this before.

'James,' said Emily. 'Has something happened? What has Buster done now? Where is Buster anyway?'

'It's not Buster,' said James. 'It's you that I am here to see.'

'Me?'

'Yes. Have you any idea how worried I've been about you?'

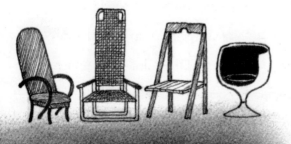

'Why?' said Emily.

'What on earth were you doing yesterday with that "little old lady" in the Starburst Ballroom? You told the security guard she was your grandmother. Why?'

'Oh, that was Morris Flipwinkle. I was bringing him back here for questioning . . .'

'Morris Flipwinkle?' interrupted James. 'Do you know who he is?'

'Yes, he plays the Wurlitzer at the Starburst Ballroom.'

'No – well – yes, he does, but he is wanted for the Starburst Ballroom murder. And given the CCTV footage I saw this morning, he is also now one of the main suspects in the Bond Street diamond robbery.'

'You've got it wrong – Morris isn't a murderer or a jewel thief,' said Emily.

'Listen,' said James. 'What we know is this: Johnny Carmichael, otherwise known as The Maestro, was the mastermind behind the diamond robbery. I believe he was murdered by his accomplice, who, it appears, was Morris Flipwinkle. I suspect Morris bumped off Johnny Carmichael so that he could keep the diamond for himself.'

'He wouldn't do any of those things,' said Emily.

'Hear me out,' said Detective Cardwell. 'The clothes Morris was wearing when he was pretending to be your granny are exactly the same as those worn by one of the jewel thieves.'

'But that's impossible,' said Emily, confused. 'I found them in . . .'

At that moment Morris Flipwinkle came into the kitchen. His wing had been well and truly slept on, so that from where James was standing at the stove he couldn't see it at all.

'Is your name Morris Flipwinkle?' asked Detective Cardwell.

'Please, James,' said Emily, 'I can explain.'

Morris let out a terrified squeak.

'Yes,' he said.

'Morris Flipwinkle,' said Detective Cardwell. 'I am arresting you on suspicion of robbery and of the murder of Johnny Carmichael. You do not have to say anything but . . .'

Morris went whiter than white. He started to sway back and forth then fainted face down on the dog basket.

It was only then that Detective Cardwell saw Morris's one and only wing.

'He's a fairy,' said the detective.

'Yes,' said Emily, bending down beside Morris. 'That's what I was trying to tell you. And Edie Girdle, the fortune-teller, the other fairy with only one wing, read Morris's palm and she said he couldn't murder a wombat and definitely not a human.'

Doughnut rushed down the stairs barking, and finding Morris in his basket, began to lick his face. One doesn't want to be rude about a dog, that would never do, but it would be true to say that Doughnut had the most dreadful bad breath. Fairy dog treats had done little to sort it out. It was so bad that one whiff of it was enough to bring the fainting fairy to his senses. Emily was helping a wobbly Morris Flipwinkle to his feet when Fidget sauntered into the kitchen wearing a rather becoming dressing gown and matching monogrammed slippers. The smell of grilled kippers had called him from sleep. He almost purred as he saw them sitting waiting for him on a plate.

'Good morning, good morning,' he said, giving Morris a pat on the back. 'Sleep well, old clam? Jimmy!' he said. 'What are you doing here?'

'I flew up to rescue Emily from the clutches of a suspected criminal.'

'Why?' asked Fidget, taking his kippers to the table. 'Emily isn't in need of rescuing. If she was, you'd have been the first person I'd have called. What's going on, my old mackerel?'

Everyone listened as James explained about the CCTV footage that had brought him to Puddliepool again.

'The footage showed Emily going into a cupboard,' he said, 'and later the same camera picked up a large woman in a day-glo vest . . .'

'Oh, oh, wait,' said Emily. 'One of the villains who smashed Edie's crystal ball was wearing a day-glo vest. We think they did it to stop Edie seeing who the murderer is.'

Fidget said, 'Emily has an idea who it is.'

'Sort of. I'm not absolutely sure about the murder or the robbery. But I think I might have worked out who kidnapped Billy Buckle . . . I think it was Blinky Belvale.'

'And I think,' said Fidget, 'that I might have discovered where Billy is, though how he got there is a pilchard of a puzzle.'

'Who's Blinky Belvale?' asked James.

'The king prawn,' said Fidget. 'The owner of the Starburst Amusement Park.'

'He's trying to make Mr Trickett sell the ballroom to him – by hook or by crook,' explained Emily.

'Crook, I would say, and a big crook at that,' said Fidget. 'Go on, my little ducks, tell Jimmy what you worked out.'

'Blinky Belvale is better known to you as the shape-shifting Bog-Eyed Loader ogre from the Valley of Doom.'

'No! What is he up to?' said James.

'A good question, my old tuna,' replied Fidget. 'One I may have the answer to.'

'Well, what is it?' said James.

'It's big, very big,' said Fidget.

But before he could say another word, there was a cry from upstairs and the magic lamp ran into the kitchen.

'Quickly!' it said. 'Oh, dear mistress, come quickly. Primrose is stuck in the shop – her head is touching the ceiling, she can't get back up the stairs to her room or down the stairs to the kitchen. She is just TOO BIG.'

There was another cry for help and this one sounded as if it came from Buster.

'Don't panic,' said the magic lamp, jumping up and down.

'Where's Buster?' asked James.

'That's the thing,' said the magic lamp, throwing its arms into the air. 'Primrose is sitting on him! DON'T PANIC! NO ONE PANIC!'

Chapter Twenty-One

rimrose had shot up in a matter of minutes, as only a giant's daughter can. It was a mega growing spurt. She was now so tall that her entire body took up most of the shop. Her arms had nowhere to move, her head was bent, her knees were higher than the curious cabinets. Her hands were pressing against the ceiling – which was groaning in an alarming way. In fact every nook and cranny was stuffed full of Primrose or Primrose's dress so that there was no room for her to even wriggle.

'Well, frazzle my whiskers,' said Fidget. To the others gathered at the top of the stairs to the kitchen he whispered, 'This is what I've been worried about all along.'

'I want my daddy,' said Primrose. 'I don't belong here. I don't fit in.'

'It's all right,' said Emily, and was puzzled why she had said that when it clearly wasn't.

'I want to go home,' said Primrose.

'Hold on,' said James. 'We'll sort something out.'

'Help,' came a mournful voice.

Buster's shoes could be seen sticking out from underneath Primrose's skirt.

'Perhaps,' called Edie from the upstairs landing, 'we should ring the fire brigade. They would know what to do.'

'No,' said James. 'It would be very hard to explain how we come to have a giant girl stuck in the shop.'

'You have a point, love.'

'Well, if she grows any larger,' said Morris Flipwinkle, 'and pushes on the ceiling any more, the shop will split apart.'

'Oh dear,' said Emily. 'This is getting worse and worse.'

'Do something!' shouted Buster. 'I am being squashed and I can't breathe.'

'Yes, do something,' echoed the lamp, running between Primrose's feet. 'Do something. Oh, sweet mistress, what do we do?'

Primrose started to cry. Huge tears fell on to the wooden floor.

'Please stop,' said Emily. 'You will drown Buster if you keep crying.'

But everything that was said to Primrose just made matters worse. It was like being indoors with a sprinkler on.

'Water is bad for the wooden floor,' said the magic lamp. 'It takes off the polish and swells the parquet. Oh, do stop, Primrose. Try to think of something cheerful.'

'Help!' shouted Buster. 'I am now drowning as well as not breathing.'

'Ah-ha. Got it,' said James Cardwell, and caught hold of the lamp by its handle. 'You do spells. You can make Primrose smaller.'

'No, no, wait a mo!' said the lamp. 'I haven't used that spell for a millennium, maybe more.'

'What about when I . . . ?' came Buster's muffled voice.

'That was different,' interrupted the magic lamp. 'And bunnies were involved.'

'We have no choice,' said Fidget. He was holding up the hem of his dressing gown and his monogrammed slippers were ruined.

'What if it goes wrong?' said the lamp. 'I can't be held responsible.'

'Pull yourself together,' said James. 'Are you magic or not? Just shrink Primrose and save the shop – and Buster – before we are all swept away in a flood of tears.'

Another nasty groan came from the beams in the ceiling.

'Please, please, dear magic lamp. Only please hurry,' said Emily.

'For you, sweet mistress, I will try. But don't blame me if it goes wrong.'

'OK,' they all shouted.

There was a moment when nothing much seemed to happen. Then the magic lamp's tummy puffed out and became all shiny. Pink smoke poured from its spout, slowly filling the shop.

'Why is it always pink smoke?' said James. 'Why can't it be blue, green or yellow for a change?'

'Because pink is what is needed for this spell. It isn't all about colour schemes, you know.'

The lamp clicked its fingers and stamped its Moroccan slippers. Instantly the smoke cleared, but now all that could be seen was a rather squashed Buster sitting in a puddle. Primrose had disappeared.

'Oh no,' said Emily. 'What have you done with her?'

'This isn't my fault so don't go blaming me,' said the magic lamp. 'I did what I had to do. I had no choice.'

'Quiet,' said Fidget. 'Primrose, are you here?'

'Hello,' came a tiny voice, and Primrose came out from behind the counter.

She was no taller than the magic lamp itself.

'Oh dear,' said Emily.

'Buddleia,' said James.

'Fishpaste,' said Fidget.

'Ta-rah!' said the magic lamp. 'Again I've saved the day! Better by far that she's this size than enormous and destroying the shop.'

There was truth in what the lamp said.

'What happened?' asked Primrose. 'Why are you all giants and now I'm not?'

Emily bent down and picked her up.

'Aah,' said Edie. 'Isn't she lovely? A right little doll.'

Primrose smiled. 'I don't mind, honestly I don't, as long as I can still sing in the contest. I can, can't I?'

'Yes, love, I'm sure you can,' said Edie, who wasn't sure at all.

'I'm sorry to leave you with the mess,' said Detective Cardwell, looking at an incoming message on his mobile. 'I have to go to Puddliepool Police Station.'

James opened the front door to find a smartly dressed lady standing there.

'Hello,' she said. 'Are you a detective agency?'

'We are, madam,' said James as he left. 'This gentleman will help you with your enquiry.'

'Yes,' said Fidget. 'We are Wings & Co.'

'Really? Well, you see all sorts in my line of business. I had a guest once who used to dress up as a cat. He was just here for the summer season. His costume wasn't as good as yours. Anyway, I'm not here about him.'

'You couldn't come back later? We're about to go out,' said Fidget.

'Look, love, I'm that worried and none of what I'm worried about seems to belong to the world as I understand it. My name is Betty Sutton, I'm the landlady of the Mermaid Hotel.'

'You're Edie's friend,' said Emily.

'Yes – and how do you know that?'

'Because Edie is here.'

'No – never! Get away with you,' said Betty. 'Has she come to tell you about Blinky Belvale?'

Chapter Twenty-Two

'L end me your trainers,' said Cheryl to The Toad.

'Not again,' said The Toad. 'They're my favourites. And when you borrowed them on Wednesday, you made them really smelly.'

'Give them to me.'

'Why?'

'Because my army boots are hurting my bunions,' said Cheryl.

'But, sis,' pleaded The Toad. 'I need the flashing red lights down there in the ghost train. It's dark.'

Now, it is an odd thing, but some people in this world don't believe in magic no matter how much proof you give them. Cheryl and The Toad had never believed. As far as they were concerned magic was for sissies. But the strange part is that The Toad was quite prepared to be scared pantless by the idea that the ghost train was haunted.

'It's dead creepy down there,' he said to his sister that morning. 'You know the huge waxwork the boss has put in? It's well haunted.'

'Prat,' said Cheryl.

'I saw its eyes blink and its leg twitch.'

'You saw all that in the dark?'

'No – when I flashed my torch at it.'

'Rubbish,' said Cheryl.

'I swear,' replied The Toad, 'on . . . on my teddy bear's life, that waxwork moved.'

Cheryl gave him a clip round the ear.

'What was that for?' said The Toad, his bubblegum bursting around his mouth.

'Because, you muppet,' Cheryl lowered her voice, 'you are supposed to be looking for you-know-what down there.'

'Well, the you-know-what isn't in the you-know-where. And I'm . . .'

The Toad didn't finish because Cheryl had grabbed both of his legs, turned him upside down and lifted him

into the air so that his packets of gum fell out of his pockets.

'Now you listen to me,' she said, swinging him from side to side. 'You are supposed to be down there looking for that . . .'

'Mouse,' said The Toad feebly.

From his position he was face to face with it.

'Where?' said Cheryl.

'Behind you. Under your chair.'

'I hate mice,' replied Cheryl, turning to have a look.

The mouse in question was cleaning its whiskers. It had oddly round eyes and, strange as it might sound, Cheryl thought it seemed to be listening.

She let go of The Toad so suddenly that he fell with a loud crash to the floor, and charged at the mouse. But the mouse was too quick, and retreated to its mouse hole in the skirting board.

When Cheryl looked up, The Toad was picking up the packets of gum.

'You find that diamond,' she hissed, 'or it will be my boot you feel and your teddy won't save you this time.'

'Cheryl,' came the voice of Blinky Belvale. 'In here –
now.'

Blinky Belvale's office window was wide open as usual
and papers were blowing around in the wind. Blinky wasn't
in a good mood.

'What's going on, Cheryl?' he said. 'What exactly is The
Toad looking for down in my ghost train?'

Cheryl felt slightly too hot under her day-glo vest.
How could he know? The door to the outer office had
been closed. He couldn't have overheard what she and
The Toad were saying.

'And,' said Blinky, 'what did your little brother mean
when he swore on his teddy bear's life?'

'Nothing, Mr B,' said Cheryl. Now she was really
worried that the other room was bugged. 'Nothing . . .
much.'

'Don't you nothing me,' said Blinky. 'What is it that he
can't find?'

'Just an old diamond, Mr B.'

'Oh,' said Blinky. 'Well, why didn't you say so in the
first place?'

'I was about to report, Mr B, that The Toad saw someone in the ghost train.'

'Toad,' shouted Blinky. 'Who did you see?'

The Toad slouched into the office. 'A great big cat, Mr B. The same one you saw at the Starburst Ballroom.'

'Why didn't you catch him?'

'It's really spooky down there, Mr B, what with the skeletons and such, and, well . . .' His voice trailed off.

'Listen to me, both of you. Just make sure that neither the cat nor that flying boy come anywhere near the ghost train. Just keep them out of my amusement park, all right?'

Chapter Twenty-Three

'I have a medical condition if you must know,' said Fidget to the man at the ticket office at the Starburst Amusement Park. 'And I am the guardian of these two children.'

Buster and Emily were standing either side of Fidget, Emily holding the magic lamp under her arm.

'Get away with you,' said the ticket man. 'You are a cat. Come on, stop wasting my time. Move along, you three.'

'Wait, please,' said Emily. 'How do you know he's a cat?'

'Because,' said the ticket man, 'he looks like a cat.'

'Do cats talk?' asked Emily.

'No,' said the ticket man.

'Do cats wear hats?'

'No,' said the ticket man.

'Do cats wear spats?'

'Probably not,' said the ticket man.

'Then what makes you think he's a cat?' asked Emily.

'Put like that you have a point.' He handed Emily
the three plastic bracelets that would let them into the
Starburst Amusement Park. 'Enjoy,' he said.

Once in the park Buster almost forgot the reason they
were there. Before him was the choice of three glorious
roller-coaster rides, each of them higher than the last.
It was almost too much to bear that he was not to go on
at least one of them.

Half in a dream, lost in whirls and screams, he began to
wander off until he felt Fidget's firm paw on his shoulder.

'Remember why we're here,' said Fidget.

'Just one go,' said Buster. 'That's all I want. One go
and . . .'

'No,' said Fidget.

Buster sighed.

'No,' said Fidget.

'Not the roller coaster, then,' said Buster. 'But what
about that?'

He pointed at a rocket-like tower that shot people high up into the air before letting them plunge safely back down to earth.

'No,' said Fidget again. 'Just the ghost train and that's all.'

They passed merry-go-rounds, dodgem cars, booths where you could throw balls at coconuts, stalls that sold candyfloss, sticks of rock and ice cream. Even Fidget found himself somewhat distracted by the smell of fish and chips.

'Come on,' said Emily. 'We're here to solve a crime.'

'Quite right, my little ducks,' said Fidget, straightening his blazer as they arrived at the ghost train.

Over the entrance a sign read:

PREPARE TO MEET THY DOOM

It was the most run down of all the rides and they were surprised to find a long queue.

One little lad was saying, 'Will we see the big scary giant again, Mummy?'

Emily nudged Fidget. 'Did you hear that? No wonder the ride is so popular.'

'This looks really boring,' said Buster. 'Trust us to have to go on a ride for babies.'

'Yippee,' said the magic lamp, kicking its little legs in excitement. 'Dear, sweet mistress, what a treat! It's so good to get out, and a ghost train – oh, what joy. It puts a shiver in the shine.'

The car they were given was red, with a monster's face. Fidget sat in the front with Emily beside him and the magic lamp next to her while Buster sulked in the back.

'For babies,' he muttered under his breath.

A bell rang and with a jolt the car moved off up a little railway track and crashed through double doors. A ghost whistled down on them and Buster stifled a scream.

'I don't know,' he said, as they whizzed through a curtain of cobweb, 'if this is such a good idea.'

'Now, keep your eyes open,' said Fidget, as the bicycling corpses flashed into view. 'Look out for the iron cage with a waxwork in it.'

'This is wonderful!' shouted the magic lamp, standing

up and holding on to the bar at the front with its tiny hands. 'Dear mistress, do tell me, are there vampires? Are there ghoulies and gremlins?'

A headless rider rushed towards them as they charged through gates to a dungeon. Buster was now hunched down in the back, his eyes tightly shut.

'I don't think,' he said, above the sound of screaming vampires, 'that children should be taken on this ride. It should have a zombie warning. It's enough to give you nightmares.'

The castle doors closed behind them and they found themselves hurtling into a huge cavern in the middle of which stood a steel cage.

'There! The waxwork,' shouted Fidget. 'Look, the legs are twitching!'

'It *is* Billy Buckle,' cried Emily. 'How did Blinky Belvale get him down here? How are we going to get him out?'

They shot through the dungeon doors into the open. 'At least that horror is over,' said Buster, sitting up at the sight of the roller coaster.

But it wasn't. Down a dip they plunged and back into the ghastly cavern. There was the cage and this time flashes lit up the huge figure.

'There he is again – Billy, my old mate,' said Fidget.

The cage went dark and they crashed out into the sunlight. The ride was over.

It was only as Emily and Fidget were about to climb out of the car that they noticed that the magic lamp was missing.

'Oh no,' said Emily. 'You don't think it fell out?'

'What a thought,' said Fidget.

'Hey,' said the ride operator. 'What are you playing at?'

'We loved the ghost train so much that we want to go again,' said Fidget.

Buster was already out of the car.

'Er . . . I'll wait here,' he said, trying to look super-cool. 'Just in case the lamp comes out.'

'Good idea, young kipper,' said Fidget, as the car lurched and they sped off up the ramp again. 'But don't go wandering off,' he shouted over the racket.

As soon as they zipped into the cavern with the steel cage, Fidget knew something fishy was going on. It was full of pink smoke. They caught a glimpse of the magic lamp, its tummy shining and its Moroccan slippers glowing.

Emily called desperately but the lamp didn't seem to hear her above the noise of screeching ghouls.

'Oh dear,' she said. 'What now?'

'Wait until we go through the cavern again,' said Fidget.

The second time round, the ghost train wasn't as frightening as the first. In fact, Emily thought that the skeletons, ghosts and vampires were all rather old and tatty and in need of a lick of paint. If you looked carefully you could see the wires that controlled them.

Their car zoomed through the double doors and into the open just as before, and just as before, it whizzed back down into the cavernous chamber. But this time the huge steel cage was empty.

'Where's the magic lamp?' said Emily.

'Where's Billy Buckle?' said Fidget.

Chapter Twenty-Four

'Shiver my shrimps,' said Fidget.

Buster wasn't where they had left him.

'First we lose the magic lamp and now we've lost Buster,' said Emily. 'What shall we do?'

'Search my litter tray,' said Fidget, putting on his sunglasses and peering at the sea of people. 'Wait a mo – I think I spot him over there by that candyfloss stall.'

Emily couldn't see anything except loads of children and grown-ups all eager to have fun.

'This way,' said Fidget. He took hold of Emily's hand and guided her through the crowds to where Buster stood, his face nearly hidden behind a huge stick of pink candyfloss. Under his arm was tucked a large doll. The magic lamp, meanwhile, was clinging to one of Buster's ankles.

'What are you doing, old cod?' said Fidget, sounding none too pleased. 'I told you not to move.'

'They saw me.'

'Who saw you?'

'The couple who smashed Edie's crystal ball. The woman wearing a day-glo vest and her sidekick, a little fellow with red flashing lights on his trainers.'

'Jelly my eels,' said Fidget. 'I saw him yesterday in the ghost train. I bet they both work for Blinky Belvale.' Fidget scanned the crowd. 'Nope. Can't see them.'

'Whether you can see them or not, they were after me and I had to hide somewhere. So I hid in the crowd.'

'It's called "hiding in plain sight",' said Emily. 'You read about it in one of my detective books. Still, I see you had time to win a doll at the coconut shy.'

'This isn't a doll,' said Buster. 'This is Billy Buckle. I think he's been hypnotised.'

'Are you sure?' said Emily.

'Yes. Look,' said Buster, prodding Billy. 'You can do anything and he won't wake up.'

'And he is shrunk. That's how I freed him,' added the

lamp. 'I did that all by myself.'

It was then that Fidget caught sight of the woman in the day-glo vest with her sidekick.

'Time to leave,' he said.

He picked up the lamp and they quickly made their way to the exit. Outside on the street there wasn't a tram or a taxi to be seen, but just then one of the horse-drawn carriages drew up and they all piled in.

'Take us to the end of the promenade, please, to the shop called Wings & Co,' said Fidget.

The horse clip-clopped smartly along the seafront. Buster kept his head down but Emily could see the two villains on the pavement outside the Starburst Amusement Park, looking up and down the promenade.

Buster sank back into the leather seat with Billy Buckle propped up next to him.

'We did it,' he said.

'If those two work for Blinky Belvale, the Bog-Eyed-Shape-Shifting-Loader-stroke-Ogre, do you think it was he who helped Johnny Carmichael steal the diamond?' said Emily. 'And then murdered him?'

'No,' said Fidget. 'No, he's not interested in diamonds, and murdering humans is not the Bog-Eyed Loader's style. Only kidnapping giants and bullying fairies.'

They all fell silent with the rhythm of the horse, lost in their own thoughts, until Emily said, 'There are no waves today. The sea is very flat.'

Buster suddenly sat up. 'Oh, wonderment of Wednesdays! It's come to me. I know where that diamond is.'

'Where?' said Fidget and Emily together.

'Hidden in the Wurlitzer. Remember, both Edie and Morris noticed that the C was flat.'

'That's brilliant!' said Emily.

'We need to drop off Billy Buckle and go to the ballroom pronto,' said Fidget.

'The only picture in Edie's crystal ball that I haven't worked out,' said Buster, 'is the seagull.'

Emily was watching a particularly big seagull flying overhead. It looked to her as if the bird was following them.

'The Bog-Eyed Loader can shape-shift, can't he,' she said, pointing upwards.

'Buddleia. I should have thought of that,' said Buster.
'I've seen that seagull hanging around outside Wings & Co.
Do you think it's the Bog-Eyed Loader?'

'Spot on the fishcake,' said Fidget. 'I think that Blinky
Belvale has been keeping a bog eye on us since the
moment we arrived here.'

'It explains why the keys went wild,' said Emily.

'Got it in one,' said Buster. 'That bog-eyed seagull
foggled their metal mentality. And it was down to him
being in the neighbourhood that Edie's crystal ball went on
the blink.'

At Wings & Co, Edie was at the door to meet them.

'I had a feeling you were on your way back,' she said.

'This,' said Fidget, showing her the lifelike doll, 'is Billy Buckle, Primrose's dad.'

'Shrunk,' said Edie.

'Yep,' said Fidget.

'A spell,' said Edie.

'Turned into a donkey, hypnotised, turned back into a giant. Then shrunk,' said Buster.

'I shrank him. I did that bit,' said the lamp as it toddled off to check on the keys and tell them about its triumph.

'Wait a mo,' said Fidget. 'Where are you going? There's work to be done, crimes still to be solved.'

'Me?' said the lamp, turning round. 'You want me?'

'Yes, you, my lamp in shining armour. You are coming with us to the Starburst Ballroom.'

'Oh,' said the magic lamp with a hop and a skip, 'I do-ooo so-ooo love being needed.'

Chapter Twenty-Five

The horse-drawn carriage carrying Fidget, Emily, Buster and the lamp arrived at the Starburst Ballroom just before half-past three. Soon the doors would be flung open and the queue of people outside the ballroom would be let into the rehearsals for The Me Moment.

Posters of Theo Callous's orange face were plastered everywhere.

'Isn't he lovely?' said the magic lamp. 'Nearly as golden as me. But not quite.'

Fidget marched to the front of the queue, where a doorman stood handing out numbers.

'Back of the line, you lot,' he said. 'Some of these folks have been waiting since goodness knows when.'

Fidget straightened his hat, adjusted his knitted, fish-shaped bow tie and said, 'I am here on behalf of

Primrose Buckle.'

'Primrose?' said the doorman. 'Where is she? Mr Callous has been asking for her all day.'

'We had a little hiccup,' said Fidget. 'Fishing lines got tangled, if you get my driftnet.'

'No, I don't,' said the doorman. He pointed at Emily. 'Is that her?'

'Yes,' said Fidget quickly, hoping that the doorman hadn't a clue that Primrose was a giantess.

'I'll get someone to take you through, then,' said the doorman.

The second they entered the foyer the magic lamp went faint with joy.

'Oooh, I'm home,' it said. 'Home.'

'Not now,' hissed Emily, firmly taking its hand. 'Remember why we're here.'

'Yes, yes,' said the magic lamp, pulling itself together. But once inside the ballroom it positively glowed with happiness and almost rose off the floor.

'Look at that ceiling! And all the gold! Everything so shiny – I am home, home, I tell you.'

The lamp's voice echoed cheerfully around the ballroom.

The young man who had brought them in approached Theo Callous.

'Excuse me, Mr Callous, we have Primrose.'

The eyes of the orange-faced presenter swept the room.

'Where, where?' he said. 'Where? Show me . . .' Then he spotted Emily. He was about to have her thrown out when he saw the magic lamp. It had started to tap-dance on the floor of the ballroom while singing at the top of its voice.

'Is that for real?' Theo Callous asked Fidget.

'Yes,' said Fidget.

The magic lamp jumped in the air, clicked its heels together and gave a deep bow.

'I am the magic lamp,' it said.

'I LOVE it,' said Theo Callous. 'This is exactly what The Me Moment is all about.'

'And I LOVE YOU!' said the lamp, running up to Theo and throwing its little arms round one of the presenter's well-pressed trouser legs.

'Wowser,' said Buster.

'A match made in fairyland, I would say,' said Fidget.

It was then that the ballroom doors flew open and The Toad rushed in followed by Cheryl Spike and Blinky Belvale.

'There, Mr B – that's the cat I saw down in the ghost train. And that lamp I told you about.'

Buster, who was now on the stage examining the Wurlitzer, quickly hid behind the curtains.

'Excuse me, ducky,' said Theo Callous, walking up to Blinky Belvale. 'You can't come barging in here. This is The Me Moment and we are about to start rehearsals.'

'Out of my way, you orange slug,' said Cheryl, pushing him aside and striding up to Fidget.

'All right – what've you done with him?' said Blinky Belvale.

'Done with who?' asked Fidget.

Blinky Belvale stood in the middle of the dance floor.

'My GIANT,' he bellowed. 'I WANT MY GIANT BACK.'

He gave the magic lamp a mighty kick. The lamp sailed through the air and landed with a terrible crash on the stage near the Wurlitzer.

'You bully – you horrid bully!' said Emily, about to launch herself at Blinky Belvale.

'Hold that
harpoon,' said Fidget,
grabbing her arm. 'Remember
– he's the Bog-Eyed Loader.'

'I don't care . . . I'll . . .'

'Stay where you are,' shouted Blinky. 'Just tell me –
WHERE-IS-MY-GIANT?'

Emily thought she had never seen anyone looking as
terrifyingly angry as Blinky Belvale.

Buster came out from his hiding place to help the
magic lamp to its feet.

'Bring me that flying boy!' yelled Blinky Belvale.

Theo Callous stood in front of Blinky Belvale with his
arms folded.

'No-no-NO,' he said. 'Now, go away and take your . . .
your creatures with you or I will call the police.'

Emily had a feeling that this wasn't the wisest thing
to say. But Theo Callous didn't seem to notice that Blinky
Belvale's eyes were ready to pop with rage.

'I don't know who you are,' continued Theo Callous,
'apart, that is, from someone quite extraordinarily ugly,

but this is The Me Moment and . . .'

'Cheryl,' shouted Blinky Belvale. 'What was it you called this man?'

'An orange slug, Mr B.'

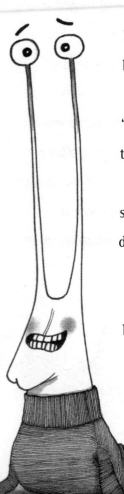

Wham-bang. There was a flash of light, a few sparkles and Theo Callous became an enormous orange slug.

'Shish-kebab a shark,' said Fidget. 'This is new. He must have learned that trick in return for the wizard's wife.'

Even Cheryl gasped at the sight of a slug the size of a man sliding across the dance floor.

'Mr B,' she said, 'did you do that?'

'YES,' roared Blinky Belvale. 'And I will do worse IF-I-DON'T-GET-MY-GIANT-BACK!'

It is always a mistake to underestimate a magic lamp. The word magic should give one a clue. A magic lamp that has just been kicked up in the air is not a lamp to be trifled with. It stood on the stage and stamped its Moroccan-slippered foot, let out a puff of purple smoke and *wham-bang!* Blinky Belvale, to everyone's amazement, had turned into a bog-eyed sardine.

'Yum,' said Fidget, licking his lips. 'I am in need of a snack.'

But before he could reach the sardine the magic lamp had jumped off the stage and sucked it up through its spout.

Chapter Twenty-Six

James Cardwell went straight to the Starburst Ballroom the minute he heard about the emergency call to Puddliepool police. By the time he arrived he found that the building had been cleared and onlookers moved to a safe distance. He was somewhat surprised to find that not only had the police, fire brigade and ambulance service been called, but also Animal Rescue.

'What are they doing here?' he asked Sergeant Binns.

'We had a report that there is a big cat in there, as well as two minors and approximately four adults. Theo Callous's assistant thinks Mr Callous is being held hostage.'

'What makes him think that?' asked Detective Cardwell.

'The ballroom doors are locked from the inside,' said Sergeant Binns. 'Screams and, er, slurping noises have been heard.'

Mr Trickett rushed up to them.

'What do we do?' he asked.

'Who are you?' asked James Cardwell.

'Albert Trickett, owner and manager of the ballroom. This is a disaster for my business. The TV presenter, Theo Callous, is in there.'

James walked into the foyer and up to the doors to the ballroom. He put out his hands to give the doors a good push, and when they flew open by themselves nearly tripped over the magic lamp. It was standing just inside, its arms raised in triumph.

In the middle of the dance floor, a dazed Theo Callous lay covered in slime in a pool of gunk. The woman who Sergeant Binns had identified from the CCTV footage as Cheryl Spike appeared frozen with fright. A skinny young man was clinging tightly to one of the pillars gibbering something about a sardine. He must be the kid brother, thought Detective Cardwell. Known as The Toad. Buster, he noticed, was examining the Wurlitzer.

'Good timing, James,' said Emily.

'What's happened to Mr Callous?' said Mr Trickett, who

had followed James into the ballroom. 'He's not . . . ah . . . himself. Shall I ask the paramedics to come in?'

'Yes. I think he might need medical attention,' said James.

'And what about Animal Rescue?' asked Mr Trickett, looking nervously at Fidget.

'I'm perfectly well, thank you,' said Fidget. 'It's just a medical condition. Send them away.'

'Me, me, what about me,' whimpered Theo Callous. 'I want a lettuce leaf and I want it now.'

The paramedics gently laid the presenter on a stretcher. The magic lamp ran alongside as they carried him out to the ambulance.

'All will be well, Mr Callous. I promise,' it said. 'All will be well.'

'Pansies are very tasty too,' mumbled Theo Callous. 'Bring me pansies . . .'

James caught hold of the lamp and pulled it back.

'Is that clockwork?' asked Mr Trickett. 'Or does it run on batteries?'

It took a while to move Cheryl to a chair and to

untangle The Toad from the pillar. They seemed to be in a trance until the magic lamp clicked its fingers.

'Are you going to tell me which one of you murdered Johnny Carmichael?' James Cardwell asked them.

'Say nothing,' said Cheryl to The Toad.

'But sis, do you think that that sardine was Mr B?' said The Toad.

'Shut it,' said Cheryl.

'Sorry, Cheryl.'

'What other name was Johnny Carmichael known by?' said Detective Cardwell to The Toad.

'The Maestro,' said The Toad. 'Whoops! Sorry, Cheryl. But I like quizzes.'

Cheryl looked furious. 'Put a piece of bubblegum in that gob of yours before I put my fist in it.'

Detective Cardwell took a piece of paper from his pocket. 'Do you know what this says?' he asked Cheryl.

'No. Why?'

'It says that you were married to Johnny Carmichael.'

'So what?'

'You never told me,' said The Toad. 'That's not nice, not telling your little brother a thing like that. Getting married is important.'

'No big deal,' said Cheryl.

'Maybe the reason Johnny Carmichael didn't want anyone to know you were married,' said the detective, 'was because he was already married to someone else.'

A tear glistened in Cheryl's eye.

'You discovered that not only was he married to someone else,' continued James Cardwell, 'but after all you had done to help him steal it, he had hidden the Galaxy Diamond with the intention of disappearing with it and keeping the profits to himself.'

Cheryl stood up.

'I did everything for that man. I hired the mobility scooters and found a man to pimp them up. It was me who broke the window in Bond Street. Johnny told me he needed a bit of muscle and I gave him a bit of muscle. I gave him a lot of muscle when I stuck that knife into the back of his dinner jacket.'

Cheryl Spike was arrested for robbery and murder,

The Toad for helping his sister, and both were accused of
smashing up Edie Girdle's booth and destroying her crystal
ball. They looked a sorry sight as they were taken away by
Sergeant Binns.

Once they had gone, Buster said, 'There's a reward for
finding that diamond, isn't there? If I remember rightly,
a very large reward.'

'Indubitably,' said James.

'Mr Trickett,' said Buster. 'It may be to your
advantage if you have a look inside your Wurlitzer.
The C is flat.'

Mr Trickett climbed up on the stage and fiddled
about inside the Wurlitzer before finding the reason that
the C was flat. Hidden there was the Galaxy Diamond.
Mr Trickett's face lit up.

That summer evening found Fidget, Buster and Emily
walking with the magic lamp towards Wings & Co, taking
in the sea air and thinking, as one does, about supper.
But that was when the magic lamp complained of having

a wobbly tummy. In fact, its shine was noticeably dull.
Its spout began to droop.

'Oh no,' said Emily. 'What's wrong?'

'Far be it from me to be dramatic,' it said, holding its
round belly, 'but, sweet mistress, I fear this might be the
end of the show for the magic lamp.'

'Lean on a limpet,' said Fidget. 'This looks bad.'

'Gosh,' said Buster. 'It's gone all green.'

At that moment the lamp let out the loudest burp
Emily had ever heard and the bog-eyed sardine flew out of
its spout and landed on the promenade in front of them.

'Buddleia and bindweed!' shouted Buster.

The fish flapped about on the pavement.

'What shall we do? It will shape-shift itself and get
away,' said Emily.

Suddenly, out of nowhere, a big black bird swooped
down. 'A cormorant!' said Emily.

In one gulp the cormorant swallowed the sardine
whole then, with a squawk, flew off over the shining sea.

Chapter Twenty-Seven

'When is a giant not a giant?' asked Morris Flipwinkle.

'When he's been shrunk,' replied Edie, putting on the kettle. They were in the kitchen of Wings & Co, making tea for everyone.

'Do you remember those guests I had staying last year?' said Betty, wrapping mackerel in foil. 'Lanky and Titch. They had an act on South Pier. One was a giant, the other was tiny.'

She put the mackerel in the oven.

'This is different,' said Edie. 'I mean, Billy Buckle and his daughter are stuck if the spell can't be undone.'

Upstairs the smell of fish was distracting Fidget and he was having difficulty thinking about the problem before him.

Billy Buckle was feeling very sorry for himself.

'First,' he said miserably, 'I'm shape-shifted into a donkey and then I'm shrunk to the size of a doll. And people wonder why giants don't visit the non-fairy world very often.'

'I don't mind what size I am,' piped up Primrose. 'As long as Daddy and I are together. I made you wake up, Daddy, didn't I?'

'Yes, my angel, you did.'

'I only had to sing you my rose bush song and you were wide awake. "*Somewhere over the rose bush . . .*"' she sang.

'If only this shrinking spell could be broken so easily,' said Billy.

'I'm sure we can work something out,' said Buster. 'I know it's urgent. For all of us,' he added.

'You see, everything in my life is . . . well, big,' continued Billy. 'My chair is as high as the first floor of this shop. My table as high as the roof. My house is higher than the big wheel. What am I to do?'

Emily had suggested, quite logically, that as the magic lamp had shrunk Billy and Primrose in the first place, it should now be able to unshrink them. But when the idea was put to the magic lamp, it had run off, saying there were sick keys to look after.

'I'll go and have a word with the lamp,' said Fidget. 'Don't worry, Billy, my old mackerel. It will be all right.'

A little later Fidget came down the stairs dragging the magic lamp by its spout.

'Noooo! Pleeeeease don't make me,' it said, clinging to the banisters. 'I have done enough magic for one day. This is a spell too far.'

Fidget let go and the lamp turned round and skedaddled back up to its bedroom, slamming the door behind it.

'It's no good,' said Fidget.

'Maybe if I tell it I'll take it on the roller coaster, it'll change its mind,' suggested Buster.

Emily sighed and stood up. 'I think I know what this is about.'

'What?' said everyone together.

'The keys,' replied Emily, and went upstairs.

The magic lamp had turned its bedroom into a small hospital ward. There were seventeen little beds with seventeen laced-up boots tucked under them. Fifteen of the keys were propped up on pillows drinking iron tea. They looked almost normal, though they didn't have the buzz about them that they used to have. Cyril and Rory were still in a bad way: stretched out, their wings drooping, their metal all floppy. The lamp was sitting between them, bathing their brows with a tiny damp cloth.

Emily kneeled down.

'Dear magic lamp,' she said. 'You have been so brave and saved the day. What would we have done without you? The Bog-Eyed Loader might have changed us all into slugs if it hadn't been for your magic. Who else but you could have turned him into a sardine?'

'I can't do it,' it wept. 'I'm under too much stress. What if my magic went wrong? What if I shrunk Billy Buckle and his daughter even smaller?' Or made them disappear altogether?'

'This isn't about magic,' said Emily. 'It's about the keys, isn't it?'

'Rory and Cyril are still not well and all my magic can't make them better. I have failed them, failed, I tell you.'

'You haven't failed them. You are their friend and a very good friend. But you're not the Keeper of the Keys – that's a different thing entirely.'

'I hadn't thought of that,' said the lamp, sniffing.

'I am the Keeper of the Keys,' said Emily. 'It's my job to make them well.'

'Sweet mistress,' said the lamp, looking up at Emily, 'if you can make them better, then I will try to turn Billy and Primrose Buckle into giants again.'

'I'll do my best,' said Emily. 'But I need to do this on my own.'

The lamp stood up and bowed.

'I quite understand, sweet mistress,' it said, and went to a chest of drawers and pulled out a hankie. It blew its spout very loudly then tiptoed out of the room.

Emily sat for a long time, not knowing quite what to do. She thought back to the day Miss String had first opened the painted oak chest containing the bunch of golden keys, and how she, Emily, had unknotted their boot laces. Perhaps if she were to behave in the same way as she had back then, when she hadn't known what being Keeper

of the Keys meant, she might be able to restore Cyril and Rory and the others to their old selves.

It came to her all of a sudden that the best thing to do would be to tell them a story.

The story started, as all good fairy tales do, with 'Once upon a time . . .'

Chapter Twenty-Eight

Emily walked down the stairs to the shop followed by seventeen flying keys. The magic lamp shouted for joy when it saw them and punched the air with its little fist.

'You did it! Oh, sweet mistress, I knew you would.' It rushed up to Emily and flung its arms round her legs. 'Thank you. You were right. Only the Keeper of the Keys had the power to make them better. I, of all lamps, should have known that. Cyril, Rory,' it called, running around after them. 'Come to me, my friends.'

For a moment the two keys rested like pigeons on its outstretched hands before they flew off again, whirling and dancing round the shop. Finally they landed on top of the curious cabinet.

It was one of those will-they-won't-they moments. Edie and Morris held their breath. Would they have their

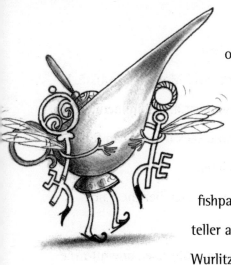

other wings or not? First Rory then Cyril dived into the locks. Each key turned, each opened a drawer and before you could say fishpaste, Edie Girdle the fortune-teller and Morris Flipwinkle the Wurlitzer player had their complete sets of wings.

Edie had quite forgotten how beautiful hers were.

'They're just like the wings of a Silver Stud Blue butterfly,' said Betty. 'So stylish.'

'The trouble is,' said Edie, 'they're not really practical.'

'Give over,' said Betty. 'I can see you at the tea dance next Wednesday doing a rumba. You'll knock everyone for six.' Emily agreed. 'I tell you, love,' added Betty, 'if they belonged to me I would be showing them off to all and sundry.'

'But everyone will know I am a fairy,' said Edie.

'Don't be daft, love,' said Betty. 'They'll just think the wings are part of your fortune-telling costume. And as I always say, you see all sorts up here.'

'I'm not going to hide mine,' said Morris Flipwinkle. His were dragonfly wings, longer, slimmer and shimmering with rainbow colours. 'I don't care who sees them. I can fly!'

He pirouetted up to the ceiling.

'Hold that tuna,' said Fidget. 'Remember the Fairy Code.'

'Yes, of course,' said Morris, brought back down to the ground with a bump. 'But Betty is right. No one will look twice at the wings.'

'Very true,' said Fidget.

'Excuse me, dude,' said Billy Buckle. 'I don't want to interrupt the happy party, but what about us?'

He had a good point. He and Primrose were still as small as small could be.

'I can do this, I'm sure of it,' said the magic lamp to Billy in a very solemn voice. 'I've been practising. Look.'

'At what?' asked Billy.

'This is one I resized earlier,' said the magic lamp. It ran out of the door, returning with a fork that was about the size of Fidget.

'I hope it works as well on giants as it does on cutlery,' said Billy.

'Oh, it will,' said the lamp. 'I've got my mojo back.'

They waited until all the holidaymakers had left the beach, the deckchairs folded away and the donkeys taken back to their stables. Only when the sun had almost set and the lights had begun to come on along the promenade did the party from Wings & Co make its way to the beach.

If anyone had happened to look out that glorious evening they would have seen a very strange sight. One large cat, three fairies, one little girl, one dog, one magic lamp and two doll-sized figures stood at the edge of the water, staring up at the sky.

'I suppose this is it,' said Billy Buckle.

'I'll keep my fish fingers crossed,' said Fidget.

'I just want to say thanks, my old mate, for having Primrose, and for rescuing me,' said Billy.

'Goodbye,' said Primrose.

She clung to Raggy with one hand and her dad with the other.

They all waited for what felt quite a long time as the magic lamp found just the right spot to stand on.

'You can't hurry these things,' it said.

It puffed itself up, let out a waft of orange smoke and clicked its Moroccan-slippered heels together. For a moment it seemed that nothing was happening, then with a whizz-whoosh the two doll-sized figures began to grow and grow and grow until Billy and Primrose were giants once more.

'You've done it, dude,' shouted Billy. 'I thank your Moroccan slippers, magic lamp. Home, here we come!'

Giants have a very practical way of travelling. Unlike most of us they don't use buses, cars, trains, aeroplanes, ships or even bicycles. Occasionally a beanstalk might be handy but, on the whole, such things are very rare indeed. All Billy Buckle had to do was reach up into the darkening sky and pull down a purple ladder made of sunset clouds. With Primrose on his back, Billy started to climb. Higher and higher he climbed until all that could be seen of Billy were his red boots disappearing into the night sky.

The following day, Edie Girdle phoned Betty to tell her that her new crystal ball had arrived from fairyNet. It felt good, she told Betty, to be back in business.

Morris Flipwinkle returned to the Starburst Ballroom. Mr Trickett would have been lost without his number-one Wurlitzer player.

James Cardwell popped in to Wings & Co for a cup of tea and to say goodbye before flying back to New Scotland Yard. He was rather pleased with himself. The Galaxy Diamond had been found, two criminals arrested and the newspapers were full of praise for the detective who had cracked the Bond Street robbery.

The magic lamp had that morning been collected by limo and taken to the Starburst Ballroom to prepare for its starring appearance in The Me Moment. The presenter, Theo Callous, had made a full recovery, although he didn't quite understand why he had such a hunger for lettuce. He insisted on there being a pot of pansies in his dressing room.

That left Fidget, Emily, Buster, Doughnut and, of course, seventeen keys.

'Well,' said Emily, as they all stood outside the shop to see the lamp off. 'Everything seems to have turned out all right.' She waved at the departing limo.

'I think we need a reward,' said Buster, looking up at the roller coaster.

'Like what?' asked Emily.

'Like a holiday,' said Buster. 'After all, we are by the seaside.'

'Spot on the fishcake,' said Fidget. 'I'll get my hat.'

FIN

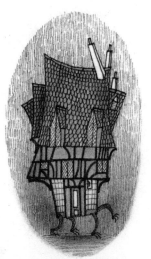